Nettwerk: 25 Years of Music We Love

Nettwerk: 25 Years of Music We Love

Written by
Denise Ryan

WILEY

John Wiley & Sons Canada, Ltd.

Library and Archives Canada Cataloguing in Publication Data

McBride, Terry, 1960
Nettwerk : 25 years of music we love / Terry McBride.

ISBN 978-0-470-67844-2

1. Nettwerk (Firm)—History.
2. Record labels—Canada. I. Title.

ML3792.N476M19 2010   338.7'617802660971   C2010-901594-0

Production & Editorial Credits
Interior design and layout: Diana Sullada
Cover design: John Rummen
Managing Editor: Alison Maclean
Acquiring Editor: Leah Marie Fairbank
Production Editor: Lindsay Humphreys
Printer: R. R. Donnelly

John Wiley & Sons Canada, Ltd.
6045 Freemont Blvd.
Mississauga, Ontario
L5R 4J3

Printed in the United States

1 2 3 4 5 RRD 14 13 12 11 10

*This book is dedicated to all the crazy,
passionate music lovers.*

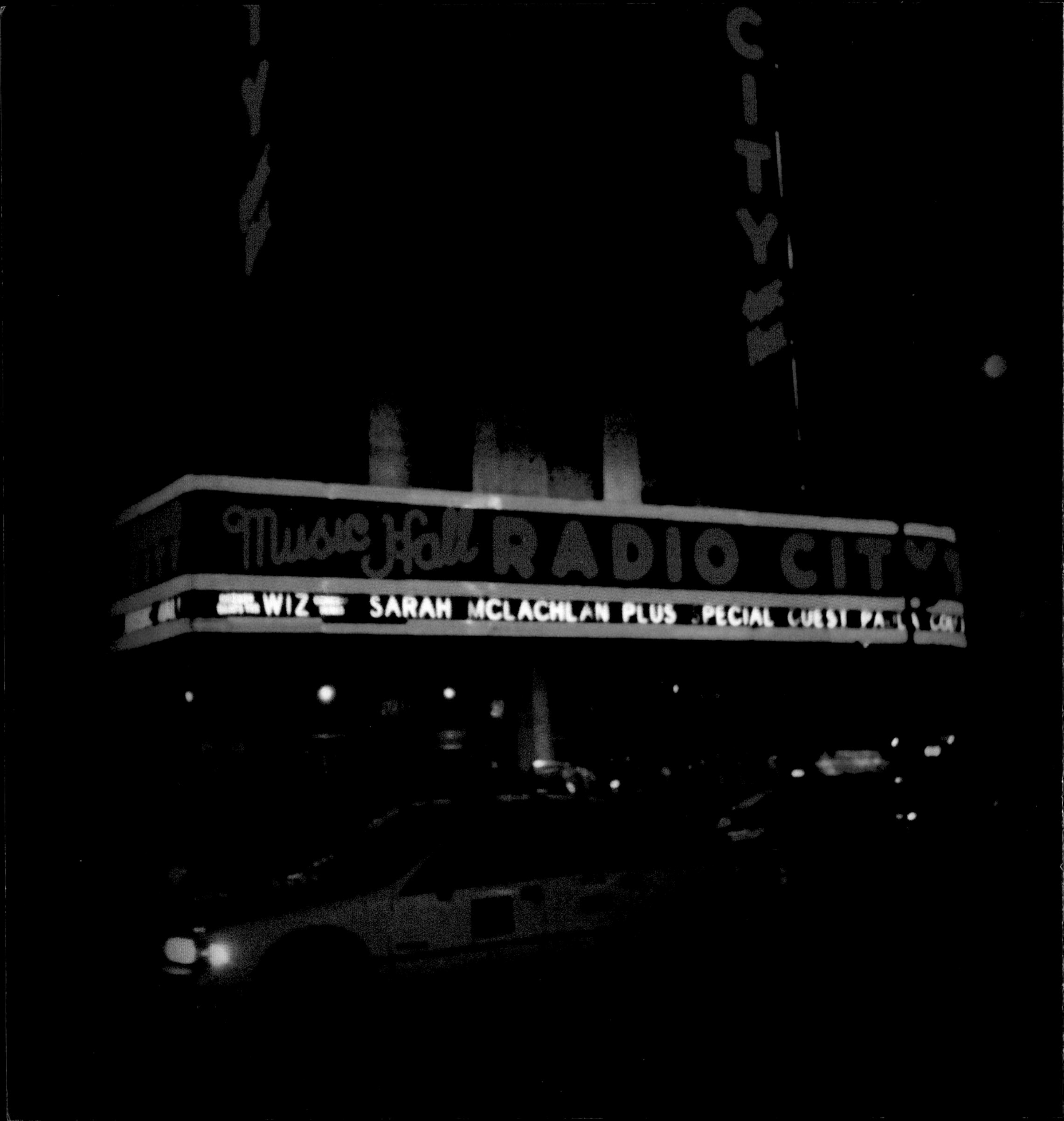
CITY
Music Hall
RADIO CIT
WIZ
SARAH MCLACHLAN PLUS

contents

angel / 2

floating island / 12

baby steps / 22

cathy / 38

skinny puppy / 46

pinball wizard / 60

sun-struck / 70

into the wild sky / 86

music of the bells / 106

breaking sarah / 114

if I had a million albums / 132

sarah rising / 144

a star is born & branded / 160

dark angel / 174

afterglow / 194

vinyl to vinyl / 198

ric q & a / 210

terry q & a / 220

25 years of nettwerk artists / 230

random nettfacts / 232

index / 238

acknowledgements

I would like to thank my parents for their patience and understanding and for supporting me even when they thought better. To Mark, Ric, and Dan, you're great partners but even better friends. To all Nettwerkers past and present, we all share a common passion and it's humbling that I get to share yours. To all the music fans that have supported our love for music. To the artists whose hearts and souls have nourished millions, you're amazing. To Cathy, Mira, and Kai, my deepest love. Lastly, to Denise, for writing a truly unique and engaging book.

Terry McBride

Many of the artists we have worked with in some form or another

angel

I don't want someone to love me. Or like me. I just want someone to see me. My heart. In the movie *Avatar*, the characters say that to express love — I see you. It's the purest thing that can happen... to see each other for who we really are.

Sarah McLachlan

our hundred people are crammed into the Dalhousie University Student Union ballroom. A whole sweaty, beer-soaked mess of them, smelling of tobacco and hash, armpits, unwashed jeans, and the sharp, yeasty froth of ale.

You are too young to drink legally, but tonight, who knows? What's wrong with a little fun?

After all, this is your first real gig, live, onstage, with a local band called October Game. This is not some rinky-dink high-school gymnasium. Tonight will be mostly covers, some Kate Bush. (You listen to way too much Kate Bush.) Some Blondie. Some originals, too.

You are opening for Moev, a cool synth-pop group from Vancouver. Kind of a coup. They've already got a couple of records. And the guitar player, Mark, the skinny one with the Flock of Seagulls forelock and the sultry side-glance, said he'd watch your set, for sure.

From the stage, through the bright lights, you see the audience in flashes and blurs. Big bobbing nests of hair, a flare of pink, smudged red lipstick on a powdery white face, a wrist wrapped in studded leather.

You hear the hoarse roar of laughter, the clatter of someone stacking beer bottles in the fridge, a wolf whistle. Feedback screams off a mic. "Hey, Carter!" a frat boy yells. "You wanna get laid tonight?"

You are all braces and baby fat and frizzy brown hair shying over your face. You are seventeen years old, still in high school, with train tracks that glint whenever you open your mouth and sing. Holy embarrassing. But tonight, you are with the band and out of the house.

Every year the home you've grown up in seems to pull tighter around you; you are cracking its seams like some dinosaur in a dollhouse. Your mother wants to keep you for herself. The harder she tries, the more you argue, the more wintry the silences grow between you. It's like she is trying to keep you from the world. She fears for you in ways you cannot fathom. As if once she lets you out, you'll be doing smack, and hell, maybe getting pregnant, too.

You adjust the mic, turn to look at the band, flash your braces in a big, silver smile. The anticipation feels like a wave lifting, bodies shifting, a breath, one electrified moment of silence.

You begin to sing, clear and fast, a cover tune. Blondie. *Colour me your colour, baby, colour me your car . . .*

Preteen Sarah at home in Halifax

You ride with the drive and swell of the band, swift, loud and long, long distance.

You've performed before, but nothing like this.

There have been years of classical voice, guitar, and piano. It feels like pure drudgery, those endless recitals, that flickering anxiety, because you never really practise enough — and knowing, when you're onstage, the audience wishes it was any kid up there but you. All those parents just wanting their own kid to succeed. Your parents, too. "O mio babbino caro." "Fun with a Fugue." That sort of thing.

Cover me with kisses baby, cover me with love . . .

Everybody is dancing. A thunder of boots, drumming.

I'll never get enough . . .

Four hundred people are with you, hook, line, and melody.

Later you will marvel at this night. How in some weird way that audience gave a whole life to you. How, for a moment, everything that was painful and false in your world fell away. No one saw your braces, or how at school, you were *that* girl — barely from the right side of the tracks. Unpopular. Especially with those Catholic girls. Always kicking the shit out of you.

Sometimes they get you right in class. You crouch under your desk while a girl kicks you over and over again. When Mr. Wilson your teacher hears you cry out, he looks over the shoulder of his baggy tweed coat, then turns back to the blackboard and keeps writing. It's like he doesn't even see you.

You hate his fucking guts.

You are *that* girl. Every school has one: ugly duckling, sore thumb. They have a name for you. Medusa. At night you hold on to yourself, lie awake and fill notebooks with line drawings, mapping stars and sunbursts, beautiful women with hair that snakes around the pages in waves. These are your devotions, your surrender, your dreams.

It's not like you don't fucking try. When one of the girls gets new tan cowboy boots with stitching and fringe, you beg your mother to buy a pair for you. You want the boots, and the Izod shirts, the tennis skirts.

If she won't, hell, you've got money too. Babysitting and waitressing and a crap job dishwashing.

Finally, your mom caves and buys the boots. Forty-five dollars. They are perfect.

Preteen Sarah at the family piano

When you wear them, you love the way they sound, so solid, so powerful and sure. You clomp down the school hallway on Monday. The girls notice. They follow you, clamour around you. They demand to know where you got them. You tell them, excitedly, you and your mom found them at K-Mart. Same boots, just cost less.

"You went to K-mart? Can't afford a real shoe store? Look at her. Bargain-basement boots girl. Low-rent loser."

You never wear the boots again, but they will stay with you forever. A perfect reminder of what it feels like to be outside a club and no one will let you in.

Tonight, you're in.

Call me, my life, call me, call me anytime . . .

Four hundred people are dancing with you. They see you.

Perhaps, for the first time, you see yourself, too.

Okay, you think as you sheer off the stage, sweaty and thirsty and slaked all at the same time. *This is the best drug in the world. Where do I sign up?*

floating

island

I have Terry to thank for whatever work ethic I have now. He drilled that into me. Mark, it would take him ten minutes just to say, "Well, Sarah, it would be really nice if this record could happen." I loved Mark. I was scared of Terry.

Sarah McLachlan

Terry McBride is a December baby. Always the smallest. He has to strategize constantly at school, where they line the kids up according to height and the biggest kid always wins.

When the bully wants to fight him, he knows he's in trouble. If he doesn't fight, he'll get beaten up. If he does fight, he'll get beaten up. So Terry agrees — with one stipulation. He gets to name the location. The fight has to happen in front of the principal's office.

The fight lasts all of thirty seconds before the principal breaks it up.

This is Terry's first successful negotiation.

Now, sometimes he wonders what would have happened if his parents had kept him back a year and he had been the same as everyone else? Average.

Richmond, where he grew up, is a peaceful suburb. It is solidly middle-class, new houses eating up farmland. A place where nothing ever happens.

In geography class, the kids learn that if there is an earthquake, the ground will shake like Jell-O, the dikes will break, and water will submerge the whole thing.

Terry lies on the bed in the yellow house that is always there when he walks home from school and imagines the land beneath him tearing loose. He is

a sailor on a piece of green, floating away from the house, the cats, the car, the school — every solid, ordinary, dependable bit of it.

His dad, Jack, broke away.

Jack was from Trail, BC, one of eight kids in a working-class Irish immigrant family. He worked in the smoke stacks of the smelter to make the money to go to university. Jack loves music and plays the violin, but when he went to UBC he left the violin behind in Trail.

He is a self-made person, and he expects Terry will get an education and make something useful of his life. Jack believes everyone needs an anchor, something good and solid to hold everything in place.

He doesn't worry about Terry. He can see the boy is very determined when he's interested in something. Dogged. Committed. Gets ahead of himself, though. He gets so excited about things that the words fall over each other in a rush, and he stutters. "Slow down," Jack advises. "Up there. In your brain. It's moving faster than the rest of you can."

Terry with field hockey trophy

Terry and his sister Kelly are like two solitudes. They're independent — from their parents, from each other.

His parents listen to the Irish Rovers after dinner. They drive a Volkswagen. Good, solid German engineering. During the day, his mother, Pat, keeps company with her cats and her sewing, and Jack goes to work. He is a marine biologist, and university has paid off. He's got a reliable government job, something that music or the violin would never have provided.

Terry knows, and he knows early, that he is expected to work, to save money for university, and plan for his future — build the dikes that will keep him safely sealed in some suburb of his own. He delivers pizza and works the night shift at Steveston fish packers. He pulls on the big rubber boots and gloves, works unloading, picking up huge sheets of frozen fish and putting them on the melter. The machines in the background hum and pound and pump, a rhythm that keeps him hauling even when the smell of offal and slime, the cold and the wet, the boats that come in one after another exhaust him.

Summers he works as a lifeguard. He is the youngest lifeguard in Canada to get his national Red Cross certification. Lifeguarding is a union job, and everyone meets the minimum standard required. No more, no less.

That pisses him off. When his employers do training, they do it all wrong. "That's not how you do it," he says.

The trainers see the kid in the red Speedo, bit of a geek, can't be more than fifteen or sixteen. They look at each other and roll their eyes. "This is how it's done, buddy."

Terry isn't intimidated. He's infuriated. He's done his nationals, they haven't. If the job is being responsible for other people's lives, well, wouldn't everyone want to perform to the very highest standard?

He steps forward on the pool deck. "You don't save someone by putting your arm around them on the surface of the water because all they're going to do is pull you under." He demonstrates with an arm around his own neck.

"You swim under the water and push them up because no one who's drowning is going to reach down and back into the water to grab hold of you."

It's just logical.

Terry and sister Kelly

Terry working the merch booth during the
Skinny Puppy/Severed Heads tour, 1986

His sister, Kelly, also a lifeguard, melts into the back of the group.

The next day Terry is demoted to vacuum duty.

Back at home his sister tells him politely, "Terry, you have to learn when to shut up."

It is the best advice she's ever given him.

He learns to shut up, especially when he knows he's right.

At night he listens to a transistor radio that he perches on the ledge of his bedroom window. Music. It comes in on invisible radio waves and takes him out of himself. It pries opens the window at night, like Peter Pan, and floats him away to another world.

His friend Dave has a job at Safeway. Dave makes good money, and knows where to go downtown to buy albums. Terry buys a turntable with a smoked Plexiglas cover. At night he carries his turntable carefully over to Dave's house — Dave's got a receiver and speakers. They hang out in the basement, shoot pool, read liner notes, and listen to songs on albums that drop from a six-record stacker — "Hey Jude," "Stairway to Heaven," "Dreams."

Piece by piece, he acquires his own system. First the turntable. Then the amp. The pre-amp. Woofer.

Speakers. He starts deejaying at lifeguard parties, for his parents' friends, the occasional wedding.

By the time he gets to UBC, where he studies math and civil engineering, he is listening to stuff no one else has ever heard of. He runs a one-hour import show on CiTR, and makes his way downtown each week to Cinematica and Odyssey Imports on the day the new music comes in. At house parties, where his friends chug beer and smoke dope and play "Stairway to Heaven," Terry drinks cider and waits eagerly for his chance to sneak something else on the turntable.

He plays U2. "I Will Follow." The yelling starts. "McBride! This band is shit. What the hell are you doing?"

He doesn't bother to try and talk them into it, just lets it play. He knows. This band is going to be huge. Besides, no one can be talked into music. It has to be delivered to the ear. He doesn't quite know how to articulate it — the words still rush and tumble in his head when he gets excited about something. He just knows that when he hears this new music, he feels it pull him away, beyond himself. And it feels something like falling in love.

baby

steps

Terry at the Homer Street office, Vancouver, 1987

There was no master plan. There never was any money, really. But everything about it was thrilling.

Mark Jowett, VP International A&R/Publishing

Mark, 1984. "We had a tradition of hanging vinyl sleeves of each release on the wall. At this time Nettwerk had released The Grapes of Wrath *September Bowl of Green (album),* Misunderstanding *(single);* Skinny Puppy *Bites (album),* Remission *(EP);* Moev *Dusk and Desire (album); and* Severed Heads *Dead Eyes Opened (album). The tradition continued until the demise of vinyl. The West 4th Avenue office had vinyl jackets all the way around the office."*

They have been up all night, Mark and Gillian. The pregnancy that came upon them so unexpectedly and rushed so quickly to this moment has been slowed by thirty-six hours of grinding labour.

They are so shattered with exhaustion that all the doubts have been shut outside the hospital doors. Doubts Mark has that he — so young, patching together a living playing gigs with a band and working at the record store on weekends — could possibly be a father.

He and Gillian still feel like children themselves.

For two nights, this baby holds on, grips his mother with two tiny fists and refuses to enter the world. He will not be pushed.

Mark feeds Gillian ice chips and grits his teeth against the dark howl of her groans until his eyes roll back in his own head, the cells in his brain slam shut, and he staggers into the arms of someone, he doesn't even know who, and faints. Then he rushes out of the hospital to gulp fresh air, to feel the concrete underfoot and try to rescue himself.

After a short walk, he meets Terry at a club where The Grapes of Wrath, a small band from Kelowna, is playing. The Grapes — brothers Tom and Chris Hooper, and lyricist Kevin Kane — have a sound. It's rootsy, melodic, with rich, layered harmonies. They're living in a Volvo station wagon, but they've got a tape reel with four songs on it, produced by Greg Reely.

"Love 'em," Terry says.

Gillian, who does not have the luxury of leaving, labours through the night.

Mark returns. Gillian dozes between contractions until the morning light begins to break. The doctors are back. Gillian has been poked with needles and IV drips. This baby, caught between two worlds, hangs on, tight-fisted.

Just as Mark feels close to passing out again he sees Gillian heave, groan, white-knuckle the bed rail.

Finally, the baby surrenders. Rushes out like a fish, wet in the rapids.

The doctor lifts the infant up to the light, legs drawn tight, fists clenched, mouth open, gasping for air. A boy.

Gillian drops back on the bed, engulfed in sweat. Relief. It is finished.

"Give the baby to him," she says.

The nurse wipes the baby's face, wraps him in a blanket, hands him to Mark.

The baby blinks, looks blurrily up at Mark.

Yes.

Sun pours through the windows like hot oil, suffuses them all.

Yes.

27

A poster, designed by author Douglas Coupland, announcing a concert with Images In Vogue and Moev. This was the first concert that Terry put on.

Mark feels like he is rocketing out from his body. He feels velocity, as if there is no separation between him, the blazing sun, and this small being. He has passed through the window glass, into orbit, and every bit of matter and anti-matter is colliding. He has a child in his arms.

The baby draws in a ragged breath and lets out a squall. "Yes" says Mark. "Hello."

That afternoon, Mark runs all the way from the hospital to Terry's apartment.

Terry lets him in, listens, but Mark can't really explain what just happened; he doesn't know himself.

Is it that he just saw his son come into the world, or has the world itself changed?

It was — the only way he can think to describe it — a religious experience. Transcendence. Everything is different.

Thoughts tumble like white water through Mark's head, reversing, colliding, cascading. He is out on tour with Moev soon, and he only makes a few dollars an hour at the record store. There is barely room for the baby in their tiny apartment, no crib, no Moses basket. Could they tuck him in a drawer?

He collapses on the couch at Terry's place.

The Kevins — Kevin Ogilvie and Kevin Crompton — are here. They've started a new band: Skinny Puppy. The Kevins stare at Mark through veils of dyed black hair. "A baby. Maybe somewhere in a parallel universe," one of them jokes.

"That's what it feels like," says Mark.

Crompton is part of Images in Vogue. Moev and Images in Vogue debuted together in '81, when Terry came up with this crazy idea. A Fashion Dance. Rent a hall, both bands play, and audience members do the catwalk. Terry promoted the hell out of it, flyered the whole city practically, got a poster designed by some guy named Douglas Coupland, and the whole Vancouver underground scene came together in a flash of fishnets, pointy shoes, shoulder pads, stirrup pants, yellow jackets, pegged trousers, and sunglasses and danced their asses off all night.

In spite of the success of Images in Vogue, Crompton is virulently anti-pop. His roots are in punk. He wants to do something more raw than dance music, noise that makes your head shift and crack, something hardcore, like Throbbing Gristle's crazy, wrecked sound.

The Kevins call themselves Skinny Puppy. Terry loves it. He'd like to manage them and put out some songs on vinyl. The timing is right; he's got it all figured out. He's been managing Moev.

Mark nods.

He and Mark had put out a Moev EP already, *Toulyev*. Maybe a three-fer. Skinny Puppy, Moev, The Grapes of Wrath. On their own label.

"No one in Canada is putting out this kind of alternative music, but everyone wants it. Why shouldn't we?"

Terry and Mark know their music. They both work at Odyssey Imports on Seymour Street. It's a small store that belongs to Brad Saltzberg, a serious alt-music nut, and his dad, Herman.

Herman's a good businessman, smart, trustworthy. A big teddy bear, really. He made his money in bowling alleys and real estate back in Halifax, but he's not a typical businessman. He's always humming and writing songs.

In his youth, he sang in supper clubs in New York. Now he's retired to the West Coast. Set his son Brad up in a business, but he goes in almost every day. Stays in the back, noodling away at a song in his head (he's even had a few published). He gets a kick out of all these colourful creative types the store brings in.

There's something about that kid Terry. Herman likes him; so clean cut and enthusiastic. He's got ideas. To Herman, Terry is a kindred spirit. He takes Terry under his wing. There are no pins to knock down here, but pretty soon the store is just as much a gathering spot as the Bowl-a-Rama was back in Halifax.

The Odyssey is jamming all the time, kids hang out there all day Saturdays, flipping through white melamine bins of records, jars of buttons to spike their leather jackets with (The Cure puts them out by the dozen). T-shirts. Club flyers. Fanzines. Seven-inch singles. It's radical — the ceilings are double high. It's church-like. The walls are blue and papered with posters, and none of the albums are shrink-wrapped.

Brad, Mark, and Terry eat vinyl for breakfast. The rest of the staff are in bands, or want to be. Good place to meet girls, too, just flipping through the bins next to each other. You can shoot the shit, no risk, keep your eyes on the albums, or say, "Hey, check out this used Slits EP." "Oh man, check this out, Dead

OPPOSITE (LEFT): *The Grapes of Wrath, 1985 (Chris Hooper, Tom Hooper, and Kevin Kane);* (RIGHT): *Moev, who continued after Mark left the band to focus on Nettwerk. Pictured here: Dean Russell, Tom Ferris, Cal Stephenson, Kelly Cook, and Anthony Valcic. Tragically, Dean passed away from AIDS in 1994.*

RIGHT: *A 1986 wall calendar that was included with each piece of vinyl. It features the label's first eight releases (top to bottom:* Moev Toulyev *and* Alibis; Skinny Puppy Remission; The Grapes of Wrath Misunderstanding; Moev Dusk and Desire; Skinny Puppy Bites; The Grapes of Wrath September Bowl of Green; Severed Heads Dead Eyes Opened).

OPPOSITE: *Terry at the West 4th Avenue office, 1989. Note the Mac SE/30.*

RIGHT: *Early Moev promo photo with Cal Stephenson, Madeleine Morris, Tom Ferris, and Mark Jowett;* FAR RIGHT: *Gillian Hunt*

Kennedys bootleg." Maybe the cute girl with the pixie cut who works the cash will laugh and say, "Shh . . . Not so loud. In the store we call them 'rare' or 'live,' never 'bootleg.'"

Tuesday is the day the imports come in from Europe. Deejays show up to find out what's new, stand there while Brad pulls them out of the boxes, Terry puts them on the turntable. Herman hangs back in the office, listens to the hum and vibe of it all, the ring and shake of the cash register drawer.

Mark plays the new imports on a Friday night show on Co-op Radio; Terry plays them Saturday nights at Luv-a-Fair. People are always rushing up to the deejay booth, going nuts over them: Joy Division, Simple Minds, Depeche Mode, The The, Kraftwerk.

"So," says Terry. "If we have two, maybe three acts, we've got a label. Mark, you and I go in as partners. This'll be our baby."

"Two in one day," says Mark, shaking his head. He's sweating now, and the high is wearing off. All he really wants to talk about is the baby. His tiny feet.

They laugh.

The boys from Skinny Puppy know they'll never get a major label onside. This might just work.

Terry has tried this before but Noetix, his first attempt at a label, collapsed. Moev had been picked up by Go! Records in San Francisco and had almost come to glory. Terry still managed the band. Now there was some money, and an apartment with plush beds on Telegraph Hill.

Go! didn't subsidize girlfriends, so Gillian sold the only thing she could convert to cash — a camera — and went down to join them.

They reeled around Fisherman's Wharf with the seagulls, wandered around the Haight, came up with dream-induced synth tunes. But the money stopped coming in, the guys from Go! disappeared — there were rumours of drug dealing and theft. Pretty soon Mark, Terry, and the rest of the band were sleeping two to a bed in a stranger's apartment in the Market district, trying to figure out how to get home to Vancouver, hoping to pick up a few shifts at Odyssey again. (Herman, of course, always lets them back in.)

Terry hasn't given up. He won't give up.

Back when Go! was beginning to falter and people weren't getting paid, Mark, Gillian, and Terry were driving Highway One down the California coast in the big station wagon Terry hauled them all around in.

Cathryn France, Mark Jowett, Paul Jowett,
John Rummen, 1987

Terry said, "Shit. We should do this on our own."

From the back seat, Gillian piped up, "Nettwerk."

She was watching the road unspool, how the white spray of the ocean glittered in the sun, and she thought, for some reason, of the French name for Mr. Clean, *Monsieur Net*. And how *net* meant "nice" in German. She'd been studying German at university. And *werk*, she explained, meant factory, or "works."

"So Nettwerk would be nice, clean work. It conveys both strength and hard work."

The name Nettwerk stayed with them as they drove back to Vancouver, and long after that.

At Terry's apartment, Mark feels like he is going to float out of the window, back to the hospital, to Gillian and the baby. What will they name him?

"We've already got a name," Terry reminds Mark as he lays out his plan for a three-EP release: "Grapes, Moev, Skinny Puppy, all on Nettwerk."

"We don't have any money," Mark says.

Same thing he and Gillian have gone over and over again. How can they afford to raise a baby, make a family?

Terry lights up. "It's not a problem. It's an attitude. My attitude is, why not?"

Steven Gilmore, a friend he deejays with at Luv-a-Fair, can do the artwork. There is a cool, small label in the United States called Wax Trax! Records. "It started with two guys in a record store. Like us. Rough Trade, in Britain, started in a record shop," says Terry. "We can keep working at the shop, but we'll make records on the side. The music we love."

Terry's mind is flashing now. Wax Trax! is licensing from Europe and building an indie label. "We'll start building our networks by using the contacts we've made in Europe through the store."

Mark is too worn out to argue. He wants to go back to the hospital and see his son. He's been away for an hour. It feels like an eternity.

He's already wondering if they will manage. Seeing Gillian's face when he placed the baby in her arms. He loves her. Maybe his parents will help with the baby. He can get another job. Do this record thing on the side. Who knows? It all might work.

A few weeks later, they are on a walk. Mark and Gillian, Terry and his girlfriend, Cathy. Mark has the baby strapped in a pouch, close to his heart. He feels

the baby's breath against his chest, every breath a note, a song.

They have named him Paul. Mark feels an unreasonable rush of pride when the eyes of a passerby linger on his son's tiny face, his rosebud mouth, his tight fists, the ones that hung on so hard.

They are talking about the record label. How they can make it happen. With everyone contributing time, working together. Asking for help from other people. Getting people to invest. "Musically, the city is like islands, everyone on their own separate bit of turf," says Terry. "I say, let's bring everyone together, let's become something unified."

"Nettwerk," says Gillian.

"It'll be our baby," says Terry leaning over to peek at Paul. "Look at that kid. He's perfect!"

Gillian laughs. "Great. Do you have any idea of what thirty-six hours of labour is like?"

"Doesn't matter," says Terry. "I've heard that once you've done it, you forget the pain."

cathy

At Cathy and Terry's apartment, there were always these cats purring and rubbing against your legs, these gentle souls. There was something happy in the air, a sense that we have something here, we are growing a business and, in a way, a family.

Dan Fraser, President, Nettwerk Management

SARAH McLACHLAN MULTIMEDIA —FREEDOM SESSIONS—

Cathy working an interactive booth during Sarah's tour, 1995. Sarah's
Freedom Sessions *was a very early interactive CD showcasing Net-*
twerk's urge to move forward with the changing technology.

nettwerk:

A Love Affair

I met Terry in November, 1982, at Luv-a-Fair, amid the lights and the music. He had just come back from San Francisco, where he had been with Moev. He was living with his grandmother at the time. I was eighteen.

I remember talking to him that night and just knowing that this was a person I could spend a lot of time with. There was something I saw in him — he had a lot of fire. He had these ideas, he was passionate, and he engendered that passion in other people. Me included.

How did we keep it going in the beginning? Terry's dogged determination. His father, Jack, was worried, dreadfully worried. He was an old-fashioned guy. He sacrificed for his kids — Terry was in engineering school — and then to see his son basically rejecting all of that . . . it took a long time for Jack to feel comfortable with where Terry was at, and where he was going.

His mom used to bring in pots of rice and jars of peanut butter to keep us fed. It was so hand-to-mouth.

I was going to school, college, and university on scholarships and working. I had a job at a church as a caretaker, I started working for KPMG Peat Marwick and later for ICBC in its corporate office, all the time going to school, boxing records at night, thinking someone's gotta pay the bills.

I had the bank card. We got the vinyl done at World Records in Bowmanville, Ontario. It was expensive, but if Terry needed me to cover him, he always paid me back.

When cheques came in, Terry used to hop on his bike and go up to the bank. There was never any money in the account, but for some reason, even if there was a hold on the cheque, Terry could just dazzle them with his smile and the women who worked there would hand over the money.

We had a bet. I bet that Nettwerk wouldn't succeed in five years. He bet that in five years the company would gross a million dollars. By the time five years rolled around, it didn't matter. We were still struggling — we'd scrimp and save to buy a couch or a car — but the whole thing was starting to work and make sense.

The heart and soul of the place was always the people. We loved seeing people develop, and seeing them move on and spread their wings. The dedication some of these people had, it was just phenomenal.

Early days of Nettwerk, featuring staff and artists (The Grapes of Wrath, After All, The Water Walk, Skinny Puppy, and Moev)

skinny

puppy

Showdown at the food table between Terry and Dwayne Goettel during a Skinny Puppy tour

We were like a band of gypsies back then. The only friends you had were the ones in the truck with you. I'm surprised we didn't kill ourselves — or each other.

Ric Arboit, President, Nettwerk

t's been a hell of a decade so far. There's Ronald Reagan, for starters, and his evil twin, Margaret Thatcher. There's Union Carbide in Bhopal, forty thousand tonnes of methyl isocyanate hissing out of the factory at night in a chemical cloud.

A smog of death that smells like boiled cabbage, burns on the way in, burns on the way out. By sunrise, children with their eyes wide open lie face up in the dirt, mothers with their arms around them, saris draped over their shoulders.

Then, Chernobyl. Acid rain. The whole damned earth is being degraded. Plumes of toxic gas drift silently through the atmosphere, slide through the brain like nightmares you feel but don't exactly remember.

Kevin Ogilvie, a.k.a. Ogre, vocalist for Skinny Puppy, calls this moment in time "the dark swing of the pendulum." For Ogre and bandmate Kevin Crompton, who has re-dubbed himself cEvin (two Kevins in one band is two too many), the darkness is not something to turn away from. Ogre says it's reality. He feels reality is something that has to be dealt with — and not quietly.

Jane Fonda might have everyone in pink spandex, leg warmers, and headbands working on their buttock tucks, but Skinny Puppy gets letters from girls that wear black and cut themselves and wonder what it's like to die if this is what it's like to live.

It's ironic that by 1987, when Skinny Puppy's single "Dig It" makes the top ten on *Rolling Stone*'s dance charts (*execute economic slave, dig it, dig it . . .*), the Grammy for Song of the Year goes to Carole Bayer Sager and Burt Bacharach for "That's What Friends Are For."

Sure, it was a fundraising single to benefit AIDS research, but Skinny Puppy isn't going to "keep smiling" or "keep shining." Not when the Moral Majority is calling AIDS God's punishment against homosexuals.

They are going to slash their own throats onstage, mock-execute stuffed puppies to protest the enslavement of animals to medical experiments, spew blood and guts onstage, and rage. Open their mouths in angry anguished vocals, lay down industrial sounds, distort their own soft voices with reverb and jagged rhythms, dislocated dialogue, and ambient sound. With Dwayne Goettel, a classically trained keyboard player, Skinny Puppy comes screaming onto the industrial scene.

Terry McBride likes them. Here's a band that has something to say. They're totally original. They're socially relevant. He thinks they could be huge.

Skinny Puppy promotional photo

Ric Arboit, his brother Dan, and his cousin
Joe Madalozzo in front of their house

At Mushroom Studios they lay down sound like swaths of paint, abstract expressions of urban industrial angst. They drop one record after another at a furious pace.

Skinny Puppy's 1986 release on the fledgling Nettwerk label founded in Terry's living room gets the ultimate pop-culture seal of approval. The cover of *Mind: The Perpetual Intercourse* — a Steven Gilmore design featuring a shot he'd taken in a New York hotel room of a low-budget porn flick on a TV screen — is picked out by American senator Al Gore's wife, Tipper Gore, as singularly offensive.

Gilmore's cover (a black and white Venus, a naked female torso arched backward in ecstasy) is the very reason rock albums should be stickered with warnings for explicit content, hidden under the counter or even repressed — at least according to Tipper and other concerned parents on her Parents' Music Resource Center committee.

Gore manages to piss off everyone from Jello Biafra to John Denver to Frank Zappa, who calls her a cultural terrorist.

Ogre sees making her top ten list of corrupting influences as a distinctly "honorary thing." If the band has anything to do with it, when the pendulum swings back to the bright side, it will hit like a wrecking ball.

From the start, touring Puppy is no easy task. They're a train wreck most of the time, and they like it that way. Bloody, loud, and off the tracks.

Terry knows he needs to bring someone on board who's solid, reliable, accountable, and straight — as in, doesn't do drugs. He thinks of Ric Arboit.

Ric does sound and lights for shows with his partner, Greg Reely. He's met Terry and the rest of the guys hanging around Odyssey Imports on release day, and around town at gigs.

Ric's an East Van Italian, named after Enrico Caruso, and unlike most of the guys from his neighbourhood, he's not into disco or hair music. Ric's parents listen to Italian music and watch Ed Sullivan, but his big brother, Dan, has a transistor radio pressed to his ear all day, and downstairs in the basement his older cousin, Joe Maddalozzo, plays The Doors, The Turtles, and The Supremes. When the Beatles' *Sgt. Pepper* comes out, he spreads the gatefold out on the coffee table and soaks up all its lush and glorious colour.

Later, Ric discovers Bowie, Slade, Mott the Hoople, and Sweet. He loves this music so much it makes him crazy — every generation needs a fight and this is his.

His dad, Tarcisio, who works the sawmills — his name, anglicized, ironically, is Terry — says, "Eh, come on. Be a butcher. It's a good profession." That is not going to happen. Some of Ric's friends know he really wants to be a sound engineer; they rent a rehearsal space and ask him to come in with them as the sound guy. Although Ric knows they really just need someone to split the rent with, he's in. The band, French Letters, wins the Vancouver Province and UBC Battle of the Bands for a song they record in a basement.

Ric can hardly believe it. The song is getting radio play, and everyone in the city seems to care. That's when he and his buddy Greg Reely decide to start Public Eye Sound, their own production company.

Ric buys a sound system and starts doing gigs at the Soft Rock Café on West Fourth, an occasional wedding, and pretty soon he's out in Toronto working the gig of his dreams, doing sound and lights for synth-pop band Images in Vogue.

But it's a small community. Ric likes Terry — and Mark. Ric knows they've put out a couple of twelve-inch records. So when Terry and Mark fly out to Toronto, there to try and woo Deane Cameron at Capitol records into a distribution deal, they propose that Ric come on board and work for Nettwerk as a tour manager, and he agrees. He's hoping he'll be managing those nice guys, The Grapes of Wrath.

Back in Vancouver, he gets the news: He's on the Skinny Puppy tour. There's a one-tonne Ford truck that road manager Dave Jackson kits out with bunk beds on one side, a fold-out bench on the other.

It's perfect. But a couple of weeks on the road and the smell of fresh-drilled pine board and clean pillows is gone. Getting into the back of that van is like crawling into an old sock. It smells of smokes fizzed out in the dregs of beer cans, of farts and the off-gassing of new polyester sleeping bags, of hair sticky with sweat, Dippity-do and Aqua Net.

"Skuppy" plays clubs, most of them one or two years old. All over the damn map. Montreal, Milwaukee, Cleveland, New York. Everyone knows what happens in clubs. On the back of every toilet, on the top of every promoter's desk are white powdery lines as thick as cigarettes. Who knows what it is cut with, Comet or Ajax — baby powder if you're lucky.

Ric Arboit doing his famous "knee mixing," 1987

SKINNY PUPPY
CHEWS LIFE

ARTS CLUB THEATRE
ON GRANVILLE ISLAND
SUNDAY MARCH 30/86 8 PM
ALL AGES WELCOME

skinny
puppy

EDWARD KA SPEL

THURSDAY • JUNE 4 • 1987

GRACELAND 1250 RICHARDS STREET (LANE ENTRANCE)

PRESENTED BY NETTWERK PRODUCTIONS

skinny puppy

friday, october 7

THE FILLMORE

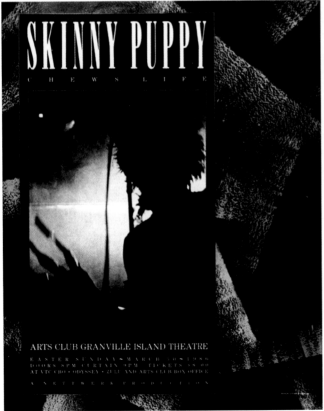

SKINNY PUPPY

CHEWS LIFE

ARTS CLUB GRANVILLE ISLAND THEATRE

EASTER SUNDAY • MARCH 30 • 1986
DOORS 8PM CURTAIN 9PM TICKETS $8.00
AT A&B CDS • ODYSSEY • ZULU AND ARTS CLUB BOX OFFICE

A NETTWERK PRODUCTION

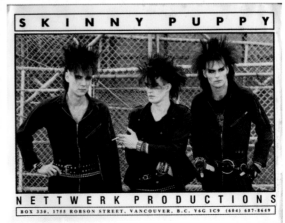

SKINNY PUPPY

NETTWERK PRODUCTIONS
BOX 330, 1755 ROBSON STREET, VANCOUVER, B.C. V6G 1C9 (604) 687-8649

Promoters deliver. But someone has to keep the show on the road. Ric doesn't want what's being cut with the razor — even if it includes girls in tube tops with raccoon eyes, girls that stagger on stacked wooden heels, flashing bruised, doughy thighs when they bend over and sniff.

Ric starts smoking.

In some people's eyes the tour with Ric might not seem like much, but when you go from sleeping on floors to once in a while staying at the Ramada — the glasses wrapped in white paper, the waxy pink soaps you slip into your shaving kit, the shower caps and brown carpeting, the curtains with sheers, the musty air conditioners — you know you've gotten somewhere. Or at least you've had a good night's sleep. And you have a phone on which to call your sweetheart and moan about how much you want to come home.

The whole club scene, the band, it all becomes unmanageable. At some point it's not about sound or music or revolution or art anymore; it's just about making sure the band is available as close to set time as possible.

It's a dirty job, and someone's got to do it. But Ric decides it won't be him. Not again.

By 1987, Skinny Puppy is playing venues with audiences of one or two thousand a night. Fans turn out for the gore-soaked gigs that have become not just thought-provoking confrontations of corporate dominance, but also the dark side of the band's own growing drug problem. During the shows, which are half-performance art, half horror show, the blood is fake, but the feeling is not.

There's a new tour manager they call Gums (he's English, bad teeth) who has replaced Ric and is supposed to be handling everything, but as the tour presses on, Terry is getting more and more frustrated.

Back in Vancouver half the company works for free, the rest is lucky if they get paid at all. They've spent huge dollars on a twelve-bunk tour bus for Skinny Puppy this time, complete with blue-velvet banquettes. The bus is so rock and roll, it's stupid. He knows the band is doing respectable, if not huge, numbers, but no merch money is coming back to the office.

Terry's got a pretty good idea that the tour money is going up someone's nose, or in someone's arm. It's not just about the money, or what he's shelling out for the blue-velvet tour bus. It's the band Terry is really

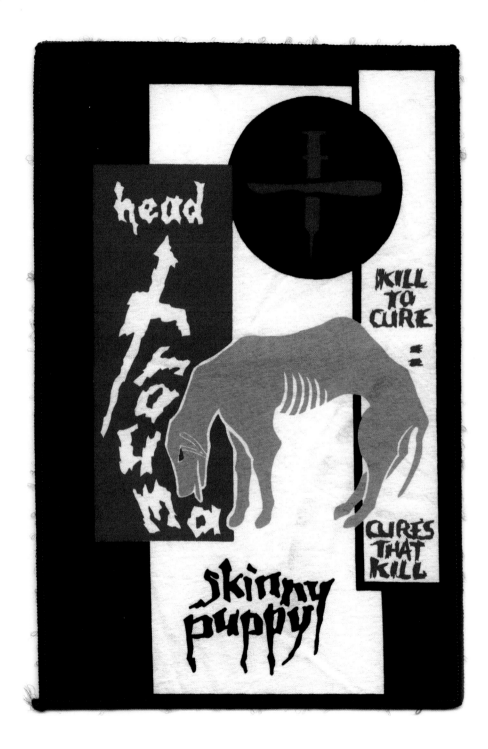

Skinny Puppy patch (tour merchandise)

worried about. He knows the road is a party and he wants them all back, alive.

It's all that lifeguard training from back in the day. He's not going to let anyone drown.

So he flies out to New York where the band is slated to play The Kitchen. Terry shows up in his khaki shorts and plaid shirt, wearing running shoes with ankle socks, looking more like a Boy Scout than a music manager.

"I don't like to fire people," he tells Gums. "I especially don't like to have to fly across the country to do it. And I'm probably not going to particularly enjoy the rest of the tour. But, you're fired."

The first night of driving, after the band has played a hell-raising New York show, their manager has been canned, and Terry's taken his place in the bunks, the Puppies stay up all night partying in the lounge back of the bus. They crash down the corridors between the bunks, slamming things, breaking shit, pissing in the can with the door open.

Terry lies awake and listens, thinks of the lines from their song, "Deep Down Trauma Hounds," about seeing "a world committing suicide." He gets it. These guys weren't drowning. They were flying too close to the sun — like in their song "Addiction," they feel the burn and burn of everything. They are *unbearably alive*.

But Terry's not getting any sleep.

"If you're going to party, that's fine," Terry tells them in the morning. "I don't mind. But I've got to get up at eight in the morning to do work that makes you money and gets your music out to people."

The next night Terry jams a wedge in the gap under the door to the rear lounge.

He locks them in.

This is his firewall — the layer of insulation that is necessary between where he needs to be and the very different place the artists so willingly go.

pinball

wizard

Sarah in her Daytons

Sarah had a kick-ass personality. I just liked her. I had no plans to offer her a five-record contract. What I've learned since then is that personality matters. It's all about who you are. Sarah was special because she was herself. She couldn't be anyone else.

Terry McBride, CEO, Nettwerk Music Group

Young Sarah

t feels good to be back in Canada. The night is warm, but Halifax is wrapped in sea fog that rolls in off the Atlantic.

Skinny Puppy is playing the Club Flamingo. The Flamingo is an all-ages club, one of those long, cavernous spaces that's painted black, and a major hangout for Halifax kids. It's pretty much where the underground scene is, although lately the owner has been trying to make some real money, bringing in more mainstream acts like the Wailers and Leonard Cohen.

They'll show up for Skinny Puppy, though. Terry walks out, checks the marquee. Goth kids are already gathering in the fog across the street, their limbs black and spidery, leaning back against the lamp post on the foggy street, sitting on the curb smoking. Back in the lobby, Terry's got the merch table all set up just the way he likes it, just so. T-shirts, cassettes and records, posters on blueprint paper. Those blueprint posters Terry's girlfriend, Cathy, makes are where they make all their money. He knows exactly how much there is to sell. They're making money again now that Gums is gone, and the guys are behaving, mostly.

Terry refolds a shirt, straightens a stack of cassettes.

When the girl walks in out of the fog, she smiles, looks around, looks right past Terry, then back at him.

"Sarah?"

She looks surprised. "You're Terry?"

He laughs. "Everybody says that."

For some reason he looks . . . unexpected. Boyish and cheerful, grinning and eager. Not like you'd think a music guy would look.

It's sort of awkward.

"Got a quarter?"

Terry fishes in his pocket and hands her one.

She turns her back to him, drops her bag on the floor, and slips the quarter into the pinball machine, pulls the plunger, hard.

She's been in touch with Terry's partner, Mark, for the last couple of years, sending him samples, exchanging letters, talking music. He'd offered her a chance to front his band, Moev, after seeing her that night at Dalhousie.

The whole thing was kind of embarrassing. She said she'd have to ask her parents. They said no, of course. Even Terry called and tried to convince them. Her mother was gracious, but firm. "Sarah's in high school. She's not going on the road with a band."

"How's mom and dad?" Terry asks.

"I've got my own place now," she says. "Right around the corner."

The pinball ricochets off a flipper and bounces against the slingshots.

Moev

There was enough of a good girl in her that she didn't want to disappoint them. So she's squeaked through high school, and now almost a year of art college. But Mark has stayed in touch, and Terry gave her a call, wanted to meet up. See how she's doing.

Mark just wouldn't stop talking about this girl. Terry knows Mark has ears. He trusts him.

When Mark plays a cassette for Terry, he hears Sarah in layers, in pure, sweet tones that make the hair on the back of his neck stand up. It's almost creepy. When he hears her, he can see her almost as if she is standing right in front of him.

Now she is, in the entryway to the Club Flamingo in Halifax. She's just a teenager in jeans and boots, and she's totally ignoring him.

"Mark's sent me your stuff. I want you to come back to the bus."

"Back to the bus? Isn't that the oldest line in the book?"

She nudges her pelvis into the machine and the board lights up. Free play.

"I didn't read that book," says Terry, grinning. He likes her. But fifteen minutes later, he is still standing there, and they're not talking anymore. She has racked up more points than he's ever seen, nudging the machine, bumping it with her hip, and shaking the field so the ball stays in play. She is totally in control of the game. Lights flash, balls ping; it makes his balls jangle for Christ's sake. She's playing like a hard-headed arcade kid who can make twenty-five cents feel like a million dollars. Every time the ball's about to be lost down the right outlane, she nudges hard and the Tilt warning comes on, making Terry think, *Okay, it's over*, but she pulls in a death save, nudging the machine with a swift kick on the right side — something that might be called illegal — then plunges the left flipper and bounces the ball back right up to a sinkhole.

"It's all technique," she says without taking her eyes off the field.

"I'll be on the bus," he replies.

He waits, while the fog thickens around the bus. He can't even hear the noise as the club is filling up, he just waits.

Finally she pulls the door open, creeps up the stairs like a cat, sensing her way into the place, drawing her hand over the blue-velvet banquets in the forward lounge. "Plush," she says.

Terry laughs. "I've been waiting for an hour out here."

"I just wanted to finish my game."

"So what was your score?"

"I've done better."

"That's an old machine. Isn't it supposed to tilt?"

"I've got it figured out."

"I wanna tell you," he says. "When I hear you sing, I leave this world. I want to help you make music."

She looks skeptical. The whole blue-velvet meet-me-in-the-bus thing is a bit much.

Sarah laughs. "Oh, yeah? Based on what?"

Then it all comes rushing out, unscripted. He is making a decision on the spot. "I can offer you a five-record deal. You'll come out to Vancouver, we'll help you. You'll write songs. It'll be amazing."

She thinks he's a bit of an oddball, but kind of genuine, too.

He lights up like a Roman candle. "I can see it," he says.

There is something about his enthusiasm and his sincerity, his mega-watt smile. The way he gets stopped up by some words, as if he can't keep up with his own ideas. And the fact that he isn't laying a hand on her; he's not even sending a signal. He doesn't intimidate her, at least not yet.

She figures she'll call him on it. What has she got to lose?

"Okay. Sure. Why not?"

He will never forget how she kept him waiting.

It will never occur to her that she had.

That night, Terry and Skinny Puppy come over to her place to celebrate. They drink beer and laugh. The guys are covered in fake blood and black makeup. Terry asks Sarah if they can take a shower. Better here than in the cramped bathroom on the bus. She says, "Sure, go ahead."

It isn't until the next day, when the bus is halfway out of town, that she discovers Skinny Puppy has used every towel she had and left the bathroom walls streaked with red, the floor covered in bloody wet towels. Does he have any idea how much towels cost? It looks like the scene of a crime. That guy Terry owes her some towels. When she gets to Vancouver, it's the first thing she wants to get.

When she bursts in on her parents and two brothers, exuberant and breathless with plans, her mother tips her head down and turns away. "Well, if that's what you want."

Her father says, "There's a contract. Let's get a lawyer."

sun-struck

Sarah in Vancouver with drummer Sherry,
photographer Siobhan O'Keefe, and
The Grapes of Wrath's Kevin Kane

Sarah has always been very good at listening to other people's suggestions but never losing the true divining rod of her own artistry. That's a key strength for an artist. In her heart, she knew what was the right way for her to go.

Mark Jowett

From your first moment in Vancouver, you are sun-struck.

Day after day, the sun shimmers — it is a blinding, yellow brick road. You follow it, let its warmth lull you until you feel drugged with pleasure, and like Dorothy in the poppy field, you surrender.

You are nineteen years old and sweet as a new potato. With two suitcases, a guitar, a five-record deal, and a boundless Indian summer, anything is possible.

The first night, you crash on Mark's sofa.

When you open your eyes in the morning, your body crumpled in between the cushions, two eyes stare into yours. A little boy. His impossibly soft face bends over yours, a string of drool spools from his open mouth. His name is Paul, and when you turn over, sleepily, he runs away, giggling.

The apartment is hot and close with love and baby's breath. Morning comes in like a marching band. The calling from one to the other of plans for the day, who will be where. The drumming of showers. The slam of the refrigerator door, the clink and shuffle of coffee cups and cereal boxes. The rattle of toys the baby holds up and thrusts at you.

You do things the Maritimer's way, and rule number one is not wearing out your welcome. You play peekaboo with the baby while his mom Gillian is getting ready.

Then you leave for the Nettwerk office with Mark.

Down at Nettwerk, everyone is in shorts and baggy T-shirts, running shoes with ankle socks. The whole crew. They all have shaggy hair, too. Except for Terry, of course. He's sparky and bright, like the captain on *The Love Boat*, but instead of a captain's hat, he's wearing a button-up shirt over his shorts.

"What is this, some kind of uniform? I didn't get the memo."

They laugh. It's a good start.

Terry shows you around, like another kid showing off the toys in his room.

"Here we've got this fax machine. It makes it easier to send stuff back and forth.

"Wow. I see there's a telephone, too."

"The phone. I guarantee you we won't be using that for long. We've got this. It's a computer. A Mac 512. Here's how you boot it up, here's where you put the floppy disc."

Terry is grinning from ear to ear about this boxy machine that sits on his desk.

"Good thing you didn't come out last year. We were still working out of my apartment," says Terry. "We'd have had you hauling boxes of records up and down the stairs."

You exchange a look with Mark. You suppress smiles.

For Mark, this is something like bringing a new girlfriend for a weekend with the parents; he just hopes everyone will get along. And you do. There's already some kind of goofy brother–sister thing between you and Terry.

"Hey guys," says Terry, addressing the assortment of people in the office that you haven't yet met, including his girlfriend, Cathy. "This is Sarah. Our dads are both named Jack. They are both marine biologists."

He seems to think it's a sign from the universe. That you share a sameness. In a strange way, you feel it, too.

You were adopted as an infant. Now you are adopted again.

You couldn't be less interested in floppy discs or fat Macs — all the things Terry is excited about — but something about him just makes you laugh. He points at the computer, his voice rising with excitement.

"Pretty soon, people will be able to transfer data messages from one computer to another. It's going to change the world."

You see one of the guys roll his eyes. "Yeah, and we're going to be able to fly around in jet packs, too," he offers.

"Now that would be handy," says Terry.

"There's a coffee machine, too. And a fridge," Mark points out dryly. "All the modern conveniences."

In the back there's a storage room filled with boxes of records, ready to be shipped. A mix of local bands and imports they've licensed. Skinny Puppy, The Grapes of Wrath, Chris & Cosey.

There is also a mattress leaning up against the wall.

"Hey. Perfect. This is where I can stay."

You set up in the storage room, with a small candle by your mattress — a warm light so you can draw in your journal. It's so cozy at night, you could be in a garret in Paris. A few rats scratch around, but you can sleep through that.

Terry has a slightly annoying habit of creeping in at four in the morning to start work. He tries to do everything as quietly as possible, slowly pulling drawers open, softly clicking a light on. The more he tries to be quiet, the more irritating he is.

Sometimes you're just rolling in from a night out, and he's arriving to start working on the books. He's meticulous about numbers. Keener.

Pretty soon you find an apartment. Thank God.

Mark sets up a little room for you at the back of the office. Your job — that's what you've talked about

Early photo shoot for Touch

— is to write songs. You've never really written a song by yourself, not a whole song, lyrics, melody, and all. But you're game. Why the hell not.

Usually you roll in around noon. If Mark is there, you hang out with him a bit before you start. He is something like you: his mind always drifting from melody to melody. Since you first met him in Halifax, Mark has stepped back from Moev. Sometimes he jokes that now that he's no longer with Moev, he has to live vicariously through the music Nettwerk is putting out.

He is someone you can talk to.

There is the baby now, and Mark has to work to support his little family. On Saturdays he takes shifts at Odyssey, where he has met John Rummen.

John is soft-spoken, always breaking into a laugh. Light-hearted. John came to Vancouver with his girlfriend, Cathryn France.

They arrived in 1981 under the grey veil of February rain like two renegades, and their warm guidance has been a light on the path of young parenthood for Mark and Gillian.

Mark and Cathryn both work at Avalon, a school for troubled teens. Mark confides in you about the school, perhaps because you're a kid yourself.

How the students wander into the office, girls with shaved heads and guys wearing capes or white makeup and piercings. Girls whose stepfathers had thrown them down the stairs or shuffled a hand up their shirt. Boys whose mothers didn't want them around if it meant losing the new boyfriend. Kids who have lived on the street, turned tricks, stolen food.

Mark listens to them. Their dark, glowering faces, their goofy smiles play in his head. Each kid is like a song that transports him and sends him back into the world, changed.

Mostly you talk about music, clouds, the sun. You listen to Peter Gabriel. Kate Bush. Sinead. Joan Baez. Simon & Garfunkel. He's in love with Elizabeth Fraser, the Cocteau Twins, the haunting tapestries of This Mortal Coil.

By January, it's raining. You come home from Christmas in Halifax to find an eviction notice on your front door. Your roommate had a rager party while you were gone. The place is trashed. You've been evicted.

"Fuck. That's first and last month's rent again," you tell Mark.

Nettwerk is giving you a little money, but not much. You throw your shit into your suitcases,

Promo shots for Touch

Photo for the original Canadian release of Touch

grab your guitar, and move by SkyTrain in the rain.

Halifax had its foggy springs, its storms coming in from the sea, but you've never felt rain like this. Every day you leave the house and feel like you are under a cold shower that seeps through your hair, down your back, the crack of your ass. The rain soaks your shoes, spreads like an oil slick that you can't step out of.

You were tricked by the sunny September, lulled into staying. Now the city is dark in the morning, dark all day, dark at night.

To get to the makeshift little studio that Mark has set up at the back of Nettwerk's cramped offices, you have to pass by Terry.

You're a kitten that's been thrown in the toilet — wet, mewling, and fur-stuck — and he's always there to remind you why you're here.

"So what are you doing back there? What have you got?"

You bring muffins in the morning — warm in the pan. You doodle on your arms, on the stools, on the side of the desks at the office, on the walls — great, trailing, loopy figures of beauty. These are your songs.

"I can't sell a muffin," says Terry as he takes a second one.

You rush up to him as he takes a bite, hug him warmly. "You know you love them!"

"Get back there."

Nothing comes out of the back room but an occasional graceful melody. The quick climb of a few notes, the descent, a love lyric or two.

One day you see Terry on the street, through the window of the coffee shop in the west end where you have a job that pays, a job waiting tables. You give him a huge smile and wave. He just stares back, perplexed.

You overhear Terry talking to Mark.

"What the hell is going on? She's supposed to be writing."

"She's young. It takes time," says Mark, his voice as delicate as a governess.

You know that musicians go into the studio, take two months, and come out with a record. Terry has informed you of this.

Your baking becomes more elaborate: cinnamon buns, vegan zucchini bread, white chocolate brownies.

"This girl is costing us money," says Terry. "She keeps coming in with these fucking muffins. What is she doing all day?"

"Well," says Mark, "she bakes."

Mark keeps Terry at bay, without ever letting you know. He finds more experienced musicians to work with you. Kevin Kane from The Grapes of Wrath. Darren Phillips. Darryl Neudorf with help and production assistance.

They walk in looking as embarrassed as you feel. They're professionals, and you're just, well, you feel like a kid.

It's Darryl who finally gives it to you one day, when you wander in late, with muffins instead of music.

"Come on, Sarah. You've got to apply yourself and get some things done here. Come in every day, show up, and get busy."

The problem is, you don't know how to do it. You are in a pleasure bubble, and who knows? You could be making jewellery, or painting.

You don't take it all that seriously.

It will take years to learn the balance between the golden egg of complete artistic freedom and the gold standard of getting things done. But when Terry starts to joke about sending you back to Halifax, you get nervous. You're not in Kansas anymore.

Reluctantly, Mark agrees with Terry that you may benefit from the application of some pressure.

They move you out of the makeshift studio in the back office to Limited Vision, another studio they have set up — it's bigger, more private. This is where the producer, Greg Reely, comes in. This is where you start to benefit from the pressure of the money clock and Greg's good guidance.

You're determined to learn you way into songwriting. It's either that or go home.

First thing is pure feeling. That comes from melody. Melody and phrasing. Lyrics are a distant third. You have to compose. *What is that?* Have a beginning, build bridges, have an ending.

You start listening to the songs you love, but in a different way. You dissect them with some analytical part of your mind you never knew you had. You think about what the artist is trying to do, how words work to build images, how to make less obvious choices, how to play between lyrics that are literal and others that are esoteric, how to tell a story.

You draw lyrics from images, emotions, your ink drawings, your private nights.

The golden bubble takes on a different hue, and you sink safely deep below the surface.

Finally you come up. You call Mark in to listen to a song: "Ben's Song." It's about a kid you once babysat

OPPOSITE: *Sarah in the studio*

RIGHT: *Master tape box for "Vox" single*

Master tape box for "Vox" single

who died of cancer. It's about love. The song is personal. There is something you want to say to him, that child who did not have a chance to live.

You trust Mark's ear.

As he listens, he ducks his head down, lets his long blonde bangs fall over his eyes. He cries and hopes nobody sees.

He will tell you that night that you have found the vein.

It has taken over a year, and many trays of muffins, but the first album is done. You call it *Touch*.

When *Touch* is released, they send you by taxi to the Vancouver airport. You are going to Toronto to do press. You feel like it is your first time being out in the world. A Nettwerk publicist, Tonni Maruyama, comes with you.

The day is brilliantly sunny. You've always remembered the sun in those first weeks you came to Vancouver, how cleverly that Indian summer tricked you into staying and adoring this place. So much so, you can forgive all the grey, cold days of rain; the rain that came spring, summer, and fall; the darkness visible that will come and come again.

This day is so sunny the sky seems to split like the taxi itself is plowing it open. Not since you arrived have you seen this bright a day.

As the taxi spins toward the airport, you cross the bridge over the Fraser River, the endless blue sky furrows outside your windows, and suddenly, your first single, "Vox," comes on the radio.

Holy crap.

You are on the radio. You scream. You clap. You bounce up and down in your seat, like a kid. Tonni is laughing and screaming, too. "Oh my God! How did that happen? You're on the radio! For real!"

The cab veers over to the side of the road, making your bodies crash together in the back seat. The driver jumps out, runs to the trunk, and then orders you out of the cab.

He knocks on the window, gesticulating until you stagger out into the blinding sunlight. The airport, and your plane, will have to wait.

"You are famous," the cab driver says. "I want to take your picture."

So you sling your arm around Tonni's shoulder, smile, and squint into the camera.

You will never see the film from this man's camera, but it will stick in your mind always, like his big, toothy smile. Whenever you hear "Vox," you will think of him and feel the same surprise.

into the wild

sky

A lot of Nettwerk's success is about the process with the artist. You love them, you love what they do. I say to them, "What do you think? What do you want to do? Do what you want to do."

Terry McBride

Producer and sometimes co-writer Pierre Marchand backstage at a Sarah show

The police are at the door. Again.

Pierre tries to charm them — he even shows them in.

"It's not a party. That's my Moog. I can turn the amp down. I don't know how it got up to ten. I'm just making music."

The cops look unimpressed. "It's four in the morning."

One officer writes up a citation.

"When I first asked my dad for a piano, because I wanted to learn piano, he gave me a piece of paper and a pencil. For six months I had to practise on a drawing of a keyboard. The only music was in my head."

"Maybe you could try that again, Mr. Marchand," says the officer.

Pierre decides to finds a place outside of the city to set up a studio. Driving through the rolling hills of the Laurentians, past thickets of yellow birch and sugar maples, he pulls up to a home.

A group of people lie naked, sunbathing on a slab of granite.

Pierre discovers this is the home of an artist. It is filled with paintings, has twelve-foot ceilings and huge windows that slope down from the roof to the earth. From the windows, he sees cliffs, infinite distances, space.

It is called Wild Sky.

This is where he will work with Sarah.

Mark Jowett, looking for a producer for Sarah's second album, brought her out to Montreal.

When they met in a hotel lobby, Pierre was shocked by how young they both seemed.

Over dinner, they talk.

"So, you're the guy who quit Luba," Mark says. "I quit Moev."

Pierre shrugs, embarrassed. He's worked hard to overcome that label: the guy who quit Luba, a band with a hit single. Even his family said he was crazy.

"It was my dream," says Pierre, "to be a star in an arena, everybody holding up their lighters. It happened to me, and when it did, it was like, what the fuck am I doing here?"

The band had a hit single, "Everytime I See Your Picture." Huge. And another one, "Dancing at the Feet of the Moon."

Pierre quickly discovered that getting onstage, in front of the gaping black hole that is the audience, was a nightmare.

As a kid, he had happily played on paper laid across the floor of his room, his fingers running over keys he had drawn himself in black and white. For backup he had the sounds of cars crushing through the winter slush outside, his own wild imaginings, and the faint rhythm of his brother playing records downstairs: *Hey Jude, Revolver, Steppenwolf Live, The Who Live at Leeds, The Dave Clark Five's Greatest Hits*.

"After we got the real piano, I used to run home from school on my fifteen-minute break," he tells Mark and Sarah. "Run for five minutes, play for five minutes, run back to school."

Once he's in the band, he has to down four bottles of beer just to get himself onstage. He doesn't even understand it himself, although later he will. He's shy.

One night, he fucks up.

Luba is opening up for Chris de Burgh. The crowd in the darkened arena roars. All the lighters go on — a sea of stars.

He goes blank. Freezes at the keyboard during his big piano intro. Says something stupid like, "Sorry folks. I just need a second." The lighters go out.

He pulls it together and starts again. A while later, he decides to leave the band.

"I just wasn't enjoying it," he tells Sarah and Mark.

Luba's producer Daniel Lanois has become a good friend. So he hooks Pierre up with some work scoring for films. When Pierre doesn't have work, he gets up in the morning and imagines scenes — chase scenes, love scenes, murder scenes — and writes music for them.

It is just like when he was a boy and played a paper piano alone in his room; he hears the music even when no one else does.

When Lanois takes off to do work with Brian Eno, he recommends Pierre for a gig producing an album for Quebec folk singers Kate and Anna McGarrigle.

They come over to his tiny apartment in Montreal's Little Italy and although he is so incredulous that these two musicians, Quebec's heart, are here, he listens to them play, comes in quietly here and there with some ideas, and gets the job.

With his first step into producing, Pierre finds himself exactly where he wants to be: in the music, but off the stage.

Over dinner at the hotel, Mark asks Pierre what he would do with a song, say, if Sarah wanted it to go a certain place but couldn't get it there. How would he work it through as a producer? What's his method?

Mark Jowett

Sarah during Solace *period*

Pierre wants to impress them, but he has to be honest.

"I never have an idea where it's going to go. I keep at it until it's good, or we feel it's good."

"Exactly," says Sarah. "I don't know, either."

"I never have a set idea or a formula. I can even be careless. I like to let accidents happen. Maybe it will be a brilliant accident."

Mark tips his head to the side, responds with a soft nod. *Mmm.*

He gets it, totally. Pierre can see that Mark is not a typical A&R guy — Pierre feels like the artists are on one side, and the label is on another. The label is the enemy. Mark is different, though. He's a musician. They speak the same language.

By dessert, blurry with red wine and a sense of possibility, they decide to work together. Sarah will write and Pierre will produce.

For a month, Sarah and Pierre hole up at Wild Sky. At first it's awkward. They have to talk, a lot. They listen to each other's music, light dozens of candles at night.

"There has to be an atmosphere to make music," Pierre says.

During the day, they drink tea and go for long walks, alone. Sarah lies on the sun-warmed slabs of pre-Cambrian rock, drawing.

In the studio, they drink tea and work side by side. Sarah plays guitar, Pierre plays drums and bass, overdubs, puts some reverb on her voice. Sarah jams on the piano. They improvise.

Pierre is comfortable enough to tell Sarah that she sings a lot in her head voice on *Touch*.

"That's your training. I wonder what would happen if you dropped down into your natural register. You can still go up there, but there might be more resonance."

Sarah hums a bit, from a deeper place.

"Yeah, that's it. What's going on for you if you work from there?"

Sarah is excited. "I don't know? We'll see."

The notes slide down the long slope of the glass window; everything sounds gorgeous here, clean as deep water.

Occasionally, they lift their heads from their instruments and see each other whole against the glass that opens to the infinite sky, the sky that spills fearlessly over the cliffs. Melodies drift out the

windows, mix with the wind, and murmur through the trees at night.

One morning, a Mercedes crunches up the drive. A surprise knock at the door. The man on the porch thrusts out his hand for a firm shake. "Now let's hear what you've got."

It's the A&R rep from Sarah's American label, Arista, in New York.

Arista has a big stake in Sarah. Mark had connected with Richard Sweret at Arista after they took notice of Sarah on the US college charts with "Vox," back in 1988. She was just twenty. For a young Canadian artist to have a world deal with a major label like Arista is a staggering accomplishment. Pierre is more than a little intimidated, and this man's presence in their studio is like coming before a Supreme Court judge.

The man listens as Sarah and Pierre talk him through the various snatches of song, the bits of phrasing. They have some completed tracks too.

"Well, that's it. So far," says Pierre.

There is a long uncomfortable silence.

"I don't hear a single."

Sarah and Pierre are floored.

"Something's got to have a hook. More snare drum maybe, grab them off the top."

By the time the Mercedes pulls away from the house, Sarah is in pieces. Pierre mutters to himself out the side of his mouth, "More snare. What does that mean? More snare?"

"It means he thinks it's shit."

"It's not like Beethoven had these melodies in his head and it just came out on the paper, perfect. Sometimes it's shit to start with, and it takes shape eventually. Stravinsky's *Rite of Spring*, people walked out."

"Well, he just walked out and now what?"

Someone could have lobbed a hand grenade inside the studio, that's how big the crater between them feels.

Terry steps in. Flies to New York.

He'll talk to Clive Davis himself. He's done it before.

He's got a friend on the inside there now. Marty Diamond. The guy is crazy for Sarah.

"Don't worry about it," Marty tells Terry. "Clive knows. You just have to remind him."

When Arista signed Sarah and repackaged her first album, *Touch*, they also tried to repackage her.

She was in New York by herself, and suddenly everyone had their hands on her body, in her hair, in her music.

She'd called Terry in fits of tears. A stylist tried to dress her in some mortifying, big shoulder-padded suit for a photo shoot. ("But it's Gaultier!") Like she was Grace Jones. At the same time, how could she say no to the stylist? The lady was so excited about the clothes.

"Am I allowed to say no?" Sarah was bewildered. "Why would anyone care what I look like? It's about the music, isn't it?"

Terry flew in then, too.

Marty couldn't believe it. The guy was just a kid — or at least he looked like one. It was biblical. David and Goliath.

Terry gets shown into the crisply air-conditioned office where Clive, the legend, holds court. He's even got the desk of a legend: yards wide, stainless steel with wood inlay, contracts and stacks of paper all over it.

The guy's a star-maker. A god. He discovered Whitney Houston, signed Iggy Pop and Janis Joplin, Patti Smith, Billy Joel, Aerosmith. But Arista's got Kenny G, too. Barry Manilow. Plenty of what they call MOR — middle of the road.

Marty just shook his head when he heard that Terry had bopped into the office in his sneakers and shorts.

This guy from Vancouver was willing to put a deal with a major label on the line because Sarah was uncomfortable in shoulder pads?

You had to respect that.

"Look," Terry said to Clive, "this girl shaved her head three days before we were scheduled to shoot her first album cover in Vancouver. She turned up bald."

Terry knew Clive would get it. He's the guy who signed Iggy Pop after he jumped up on the desk and serenaded him with a Frank Sinatra tune.

"I mean, it's sort of crazy, but that's just her. And you can't make her into something else, because if you try, she's going to get on the bus and go back to Halifax and make jewellery."

There is something so affable about Terry — so boy next door, so disarmingly honest and likeable, that the execs listen to him.

To close the deal, Marty and Terry take Clive to see Sarah live, in a New York show.

Clive hears her. She is a handful of wildflowers, untied.

After that, Clive says, "Leave her alone. Let her do whatever she wants."

Early Sarah photo shoot

Sarah writing in the studio at the piano

No more wedging her in this category or that, into Jean Paul Gaultier, into some unfitting form, some category.

Now that the peace has been shattered at Wild Sky, Terry's back to New York. Album two, round two. He needs to buy some time, and space for Sarah and Pierre. He has to get her a pass because she's way too polite to demand it herself.

He isn't here to remind Clive of who Sarah is, or what Nettwerk is all about. He doesn't have to. He's here to remind Clive Davis of who he is — someone with an extraordinary gift to recognize that talent has to find its own way. The man Steven Tyler immortalized with the lyrics: *Old Clive Davis said . . . I'm gonna make you a star, just the way you are.*

Terry brings Sarah and Pierre to Vancouver for a summit meeting. Nettwerk's got a real office now, with a big boardroom table, but there's a bunch of bikes leaning up in the hallway, dogs lying in doorways — there's even a toddler pulling himself up on a chair.

They all sit down together. Sarah, Pierre, Mark, Terry, Ric.

Terry says, simply, "Okay. Where do we go from here?"

"What you've got is good," says Mark.

"There's no more money for Wild Sky. The budget's done," says Ric.

They all sit quietly.

Finally, Terry says, "There's no single."

His face splits into a huge smile, he throws his head back and laughs. Sarah, Pierre, and Mark all burst out laughing. Ric shakes his head.

Then Terry looks at Sarah and Pierre. "You tell me what you want to do."

Pierre and Sarah exchange glances. Finally Pierre surprises himself. "What if Sarah and I try to write a single together?"

Now they are writing partners. The next day, Pierre and Sarah meet in a Chinese restaurant with paper placemats and pink tablecloths.

"Okay," says Pierre. "What now?"

"How about a drink?" Sarah says.

For the next week they meet in coffee shops and tea rooms. It's like back to square one. They have to talk. A lot.

He suggests something; she says, "No, no, no."

Pierre feels off-kilter.

They meet again at the Chinese restaurant. Sarah rips the edges of a placemat that lists drinks: grasshopper, pink lady, angel's kiss.

She suggests something; Pierre brushes it off.

They fight on the street, sit for hours in silence. A waitress asks if they are newlyweds.

Finally, they come up with something they agree on: the egg, birth, beginnings. It's pretty vague.

Nettwerk has set them up in an old dive shop on West Fourth. It's called the Deep End, and it's right next to the Nettwerk office.

Every day they have to descend into a converted dive tank to work. It's stifling and windowless. Airless as the ocean deep, sound muffled with blankets.

"It's too close," Pierre mutters.

Nettwerk and that relentlessly cheerful Terry are right next door. Not only that, they are always dropping in, peering down at them. Looking for the single.

One day Pierre comes in and finds Sarah in the corridor at the Deep End, her body melting against the wall, crying in frustration. "Why go through this? Why even try?"

"It does come," Pierre says. He doesn't even remember what he says next, but he knows that they are alike. They have argued, but it isn't the arguments that count. It is the understanding they have.

"Let's keep going," he says.

She looks at him, her eyes swollen with tears, her face puffy. They are in the depths.

She remembers how she brought her first record, *Touch*, home to her mother, how she offered it like a talisman. As if that flat disc of black wax, like magic, would transfer some power to her mom. Some confidence.

Her mother turned it over in her hands, looked at the picture on the front, the song titles on the back. Then she slid the record out of its jacket and put it on the turntable, carefully. Sarah left the room. She couldn't be there when her mother listened to it. She felt . . . embarrassed. It's like letting your parents know you're not a virgin anymore. Everything was on that black disc. *This is who I am. I see you. See me.*

When Sarah came back into the room, she could see her mother liked the album. Not that she

This is the photo used in the U.S. version of Touch *with Sarah's marks indicating the crop that she likes.*

was forthcoming. No explosive compliments. That just wasn't her style. But there was something new. Relief. Acceptance. An opening.

Sarah and Pierre are in the Deep End. She's emotional, but he doesn't mind. She's doing all the crying for both of them. When the tears subside, they talk quietly, hum. Pierre plays a phrase with his fingers in the air.

She lifts her head from her guitar and says, "How about . . . *Into the fire . . . ?*"

"Yeah, that's good."

Mother teach me to walk again . . . no more compromise . . .

Yes. It's a funny thing about the two of them. They don't know what they want, but they recognize it when they hear it.

After that, Pierre takes Sarah to New Orleans, to the studio of Daniel Lanois. In New Orleans, they can be wild and loud and above water — and finish the album they will call *Solace*.

Peter Gabriel is there too, working with Dan. The rumour is that Daniel Lanois has to lock him in a room to get him to finish a song.

Sarah bumps into Peter in the kitchen one day, just as she's dunking a tea bag into a cup of boiled water.

"You working on something?" he asks.

Her knees buckle. Peter Gabriel is one of her heroes.

"Yeah," she says, blushing. "It's taking awhile."

He nods. "Yeah, me too. This stuff takes time. It really does."

Sarah, Camille Henderson, David Sinclair,
and Ashwin Sood at Wild Sky Studio

music

of the
bells

Sarah has always been our moral compass.

Terry McBride

Sarah in Thailand working with World Vision

A barefoot girl lies on a mattress that is carelessly draped with a sheet of worn cotton, hair sliding over her face. She looks at the tile floor, not at you. Around the bed, on the cement wall, she has taped up photos of Asian pop stars torn from magazines. Girl singers with shiny hair, bright lipstick, and microphones.

"She doesn't know how old she is. Her mother died when she was young. Her aunt brought her to the city and sold her for two hundred dollars. She might be twelve," the guide explains.

You learn that the girls get very little food in the brothels, so they will be thin and compliant. That they have to take care of fifteen or more men a day, and they are locked in their rooms at night.

This girl, you are told, probably has AIDS.

The other girls are eleven, thirteen, fifteen, perhaps. All skinny, too.

They scatter like tiny brown birds when the camera crew comes through.

Outside the streets of the red-light district are a barrage of colours, girls in tight dresses, and neon signs in English: Super Pussy, Kiss Kiss, The Dollhouse.

The pimps, you can spot them a mile away. They hang out at the train station, pick up the girls who come in from the country, promise them work and a safe house.

The next thing they know, they're here.

And so are you. Terry David Mulligan, a Much Music host, invited you to Thailand and Cambodia to do this documentary on AIDS to raise awareness for the work of World Vision.

Your best friend Crystal — your saving grace — has accompanied you on the trip.

After Bangkok, you travel to Phnom Penh, where the producers take you to the national pediatric hospital. You are asked to walk into the wards with the cameras. To be a journalist. They lead you to a woman who sits holding her baby. He is dying.

The mother looks at you, at your cameras, her eyes filled with terror.

"I can't. This is the worst moment in this woman's life, and you want me to go in and get a sound bite?"

You are overwhelmed. The interpreter looks questioningly at Mulligan.

You press your hands together in a prayer of apology, bow to the mother awkwardly, and back out of the room. Crystal follows.

"If she had an education, which she doesn't because only five percent of women in this country finish school; if she had known she could get an immunization for her child; if there had been a clinic near her village . . . That's why they need you here," says Crystal. "It's not about a sound bite."

"I have no idea what I can possibly do to help."

What you're seeing scares the crap out of you. You keep looking for old people on the streets, but there are none. Everyone looks shell-shocked. The fear you saw in that young mother's face as her child laboured for breath — you feel it too.

It didn't scare you to move four thousand miles away from your family on the promise of a record contract from someone you barely knew, but here, you are afraid.

How could you have come into the world in a tidy suburb in Canada with enough to eat, and clothes, and a bed to sleep in at night, with medical care and education? By accident of birth?

How could that girl who dreams of pop stars, who dreams of dreams, never ever have a chance?

While you were home watching *The Brady Bunch*, someone was selling her to a brothel?

Next, the crew takes you to the killing fields at Choeung Ek. There are rolling, grassy hills here, great depressions where thousands of men, women, and children were killed by the Khmer Rouge, and their bodies buried in mass graves.

There are trees with paths that wend between them — the wooded area is not so different from where you liked to walk in the parks of the neighbourhood where you grew up — except that everywhere you step there is the crunch of bone shards. You see teeth scattered in the dirt.

In the field is a Buddhist *stupa* — a small memorial temple — filled with skulls. Most of them are smashed or cracked. They didn't want to waste bullets. For the children, you are told, they didn't need an axe or a bludgeon; they just bashed their heads against the trees.

It is strangely peaceful here.

You hear children now, playing in the distance, laughing and singing, and the tinkling of cowbells. The sounds pull you away from the guide, from the group that circles you like a shield. Step by step, you move out, past the trees, through a field, your Sony Walkman in hand to record.

"Hey!" someone yells. "Get your ass back here. Landmines! There are landmines everywhere!"

The warning voice is faint and far away. You keep walking. You are following the music of the bells.

OPPOSITE: *With television personality Terry David Mulligan; with close friend Crystal Heald*

breaking

sarah

You hit up against a lot of walls if you follow your own path. You've got to break through. Even when things are at their hardest, when I feel like I'm going through the rhinoceros's ass, I know that something good is going to come out of it.

Sarah McLachlan

Sarah during rehearsal

ou've been on tour for twenty-two months. Terry has ping-ponged you across America without stopping, and seemingly without logic.

Every time you wrap up a leg of the tour, when you're so exhausted your guitar feels like lead and your lyrics feel like ashes in your mouth, Terry shows up. With a plan.

"Here," he says, pointing to a map. "They love you in Milwaukee."

Dan Fraser, a new partner in Nettwerk and your tour manager, shakes his head, sticks his fingers in his ears. "La, la, la, I don't hear you."

"What do you do, Terry? Take a map and throw a dart at it? One day I'm in Chicago, the next day I'm in some suburb in Florida."

Terry chuckles. "I'm running spreadsheets."

He explains how he uses SoundScan data to track radio plays and obsessively charts pathways for you based on pockets of fans, flares of activity in this area or that one, until he's got you bursting all over the night skies.

"You're double platinum, going triple," he says.

You look at Dan.

"We've spent three hundred days together this year, what's a few more?" says Dan.

Dan gets that Terry is like a heat-seeking missile. Wherever there is some traction, that's where he's going to send you. *Fumbling Towards Ecstasy* is your third album. Arista has been your U.S. and world label since *Touch*, but they are used to divas, like Whitney Houston. Put 'em on the radio, and push them in a few major markets.

Big labels, they're all about mass marketing — they've got money and radio promotion, people, clout, and leverage — they push music through *Billboard* charts and deals: Play this artist or you can't have that one.

"Look. SoundScan shows the digital fingerprint of every song play. You can break a market fan by fan. Let them hear you. Let them tell the radio station and the label what they want."

You're so burnt, you don't even bother to wipe the tears away. Dan rushes to the bathroom, hands you a roll of toilet paper.

Dan is your shield. Your protector. Funny how things work out. Terry had fired him as The Grapes of Wrath tour manager but brought him back in for you, then made him a partner. Dan cares about the ecosystem around you, cares about you.

"Sarah, we've made unbelievable progress. I've even got the ratio figured out: If you sell ten CDs somewhere, you can sell one concert ticket."

Sarah and gear

He calls it micro-marketing.

You try to explain. "I'm tired. If I don't love it, it's like being up there telling a lie."

Terry listens.

You tell him you lied a lot when you were growing up, the kind of lies a kid tells with her body, and her behaviour, lies to try and keep the peace, make other people happy. You don't want to do that anymore.

Terry chuckles. "That's one of the things I love about you — that you can't lie."

He also knows that once your audience is out there, all the objections will drop away.

By the end of the night, it's like he's sprinkled you with fairy dust.

So you do it. You roll into town, do morning radio, play record stores in the afternoon, a show in the evening. Late at night in the local Ramada, you and the crew play bocce ball in the long brown hallways. It's so dead this time of night, you can practically hear the sound of the balls creeping along the carpet, Dan's long braid flipping against his belt. He stays up with you, like some kind of babysitter. It's you and the worst hair in show business, but God, he makes you laugh. The only other sounds this late at night are a TV blaring from the room next to yours, the rattle of ice dropping from the ice machine, the hum of the vending machine on the landing.

Dan's been on the road so long that when you finally get to stay in a hotel, he can't sleep. Can't sleep because he can't feel the wheels of the bus turning. He has to run the air conditioner to simulate the sound of the road.

You don't know what hurts more, the thought of the work it will take to undress and crawl into bed, or keeping your eyes peeled open and throwing another ball.

You're tired. You're done.

Still, there is something that keeps you going. Like an orange that's been juiced, there is always another drop to be crushed from somewhere beneath the pith and the skin. By the end of North America, you're playing venues of one thousand, two thousand, more.

Terry shows up again. "Let's really try and get something happening in Europe."

So you start from scratch. October, November, December. Grey, cold every day. You are opening for the Crash Test Dummies, and you are definitely the opening act. Winning over crowds in German beer halls. You're not playing to the converted anymore. This is work.

Your relationship with your boyfriend is disintegrating. You try to drag him out of bed in the morning to sightsee. You tour Bavarian castles, send postcards, drink espresso and local beer.

There's this guy Lance who's a roadie for the Crash Test Dummies. He's got long hair like some kind of surfer dude, and he thinks he's the hottest shit ever. Every time you pass by him and his buddy the lighting guy, there's some kind of comment.

"Hey, baby. You're looking good in those jeans. You wanna hit it? I'm here if you want me. I've never had any complaints."

The two of them talk like this all the time to you and Camille, your backup singer. You laugh, and smile, sometimes make a bright comment in return, and he puffs up. Mr. Wonderful.

At first it seems like, *Okay, he's trying to be funny*. But it goes on and on. It's subtly humiliating, because you can't really tell him to fuck off. You're just the opening act over here, and you're all on the road together, and everybody has to get along. You have to be polite, and he can get away with whatever he wants?

You're bound by something internal, as well — that training to always be the good girl. You have your mother's graciousness, her reserve, her manners on automatic override, but fuck, it's annoying. The longer it goes on, the less you feel like yourself. And every time you smile and play nice, it feels more and more like a lie.

The last show is in Paris. You've finished your set. You and Camille are having a drink backstage. The crew is already milling around, anxious to start the load out. It's almost over. You're exhausted. Sick. Depleted. Your throat is sore. You can barely talk.

Then Lance the roadie gets onstage to sing with the Dummies. He's up there with his legs spread apart, flicking his long hair back like he's living out his rock 'n' roll fantasy.

"We gotta do something," you say.

Camille is in. This is Paris. You can get away with it. No one will ever hear about it. You decide to rush the stage, throw yourselves at his feet and try to claw his clothes off him like some crazed, adoring fans.

Mr. Wonderful doesn't get the joke. He loves it. Grinds his hips. *Oh yeah, baby. Come and get a piece of this*. Now the whole audience is shouting along with him.

Vintage Sarah photo

Polaroid "outs" from Rolling Stone
photo shoot

You feel like someone's just dumped pig's blood over your head at the prom. Only your telekinetic powers aren't working, and the best you can do is get offstage as fast as you can.

You are pissed off. Disgusted with yourself for having made the wrong call. Your boyfriend thinks you've made an ass of yourself and lets you know it.

The after-party is around the corner at a posh Paris restaurant. You slam in wearing your favourite grey overalls, an undershirt, and boots, full of bravado and scotch. There's no show tomorrow, so you've had a bit to drink and your polite reserve is gone. You don't know where, but it's gone.

Mr. Wonderful flips his hair over his shoulder and he eyes you with a smirk when you walk in. "Hey baby."

All the anger and helplessness floods you like the colour red; it's not something you even understand.

Someone thrusts a beer in your hand. You swagger up to him, draw a finger down his chest. "Okay. You think you're so hot; you must have a pretty big cock. I wanna see it. Must be huge."

He laughs, pulls your hand off him.

"Come by my room later." He turns around. You duck in front of him.

"Oh no! We all want to see it. Now. We all want to see how fabulous you are."

You've got him now. He's embarrassed. You swivel your hips. "Come on, baby. You're looking pretty good in those jeans."

He jumps back when you grab for his T-shirt and start to tug it up.

"What? Are you shy? I'm not." You flick open the latch on your overall straps. First one, then the other.

"Go ahead," he sneers, egging you on.

"What's the matter? You're all talk? No action?"

You climb up on the table, shimmy out of your overalls. Letting them drop, you step out of them, bare-legged in your boots. You chug from a champagne bottle.

The crowd presses around you. At the back of the restaurant, people are standing on their chairs.

Off comes the undershirt. You swing it around like a piece of lingerie, one hand pressed over your breasts.

He backs away, beet red. "I can't. I just can't."

Sweet victory.

Someone gives you a hand down from the table. You stoop to grab your overalls, and when you stand up, you're face-to-face with your boyfriend.

He looks pissed. Mr. Wonderful's buddy, the lighting guy, is poking at him. "You gonna let your woman get away with that?"

Suddenly the room tilts, like a funhouse, and everything looks ugly. Light flares in the mirrors behind the bar, all around you people lurch and bray — it's straight out of Fellini. Your boyfriend has fixed you with that glare that makes you feel small and wrong and out of place.

Lance says, "I'll show you my dick, Sarah."

Dan, who has shouldered his way to the front of the crowd, steps in between you. "Sarah, we've got to get back to the bus. We're leaving tomorrow, there's shit to clean up."

"Come on, Sarah, I'll show you my dick." Lance grabs you by the wrists and holds you tight, presses his body up against you.

You can't move. You can't even see. A sound like waves crashes in your ears. It is the blood rushing to your head. You start kicking his shins as hard as you can. Kicking him with your Frye boots. Bam, bam, bam.

Dan manages to pry you apart. Lance doubles over. His shins are bleeding. Dan picks you up, slings you over his shoulder and carries you out.

Your boyfriend comes into the bus and tears a strip off you. He's got a unique way of making you feel bad about feeling bad.

You fling shoes at him.

Then you cry so hard you can't stop. There is nothing left.

In the morning, you wake up, mortified. Your mouth tastes sour, your eyes are sandy, and it feels like your throat has a razor blade stuck in it.

Dan says, "Come on, Sarah. Get up. Let's get your things sorted out. We've got to go play at the Vatican."

"No. No way. I want to go home." You say it, even though after almost two years, you don't know where home is anymore.

"Sarah, it's the pope. It's all arranged."

All you can think of is Morocco. There are four days before you have to be in Rome. You want to drink mint tea, let the hot air of the Sahara heal you, hear the melodic chanting of the muezzin calling the faithful to prayer.

"Absolutely no way, Sarah. We can't allow it."

Dan hands you a coffee, looks around the bus at the heaps of shoes, clothing, music strewn everywhere. "Look at this shit. Remind me never to

*Sarah promotional photo taken
by Kharen Hill*

let you drink champagne again. You gotta clean this shit up."

"I just want to go for a few days."

Your head feels like it's been cleaved in two. There's more to clean up on the bus; somewhere among the piles of crap, are all the pieces of you that came apart last night. Before you can clean up, you'll have to pick up your own hands, your legs, your feet, your heart.

"I have to collect myself."

"That's my job," says Dan. "Morocco's not safe."

"Well, obviously Paris isn't safe either."

"Sarah, I'm sorry. We just can't let you go. We've got four days. We'll go to Crete together."

Slowly, painfully, you gather your things.

You will go to Crete. You don't know why you are still a good little girl, still listening to everybody.

On the plane, you can barely look at Dan, you're so embarrassed.

He tries to make you feel better, tells you, heck, you're young. It was a difficult situation that built up, and he would have done the same thing if it had been him.

"You grow up in steps, Sarah. We all do."

There wasn't anything wrong with what you did, you were just having fun. But somehow everything has gone sideways and you feel like the biggest asshole in the world.

Crete is grey, cloudy, and cold. It's off-season, you're a vegetarian and there's no fish, or tomatoes, no lemon. Just oily meat stews spiked with oregano, potatoes swimming in fat. And Dan. You still can't look at him.

Most of the restaurants are shuttered for the winter, and there's nothing for you and Dan to do but sit in your rooms or across the table from each other. You have laryngitis, so at least you have a reason not to talk.

You arrive at the Vatican where you will sing for the papal Christmas concert. You go straight to rehearsal with the Vatican symphony orchestra, and sing the Christmas carol you've been asked to learn, "Oh, Little Town of Bethlehem." Well, hell, you've been singing it your whole life. What's to learn?

But you've never sung with a symphony before. The conductor is always a half-bar ahead of the first violinist you are standing next to; he moves his wand this way, while the violinist goes that way. There are no drums and you have no idea who to follow.

Photo from album shoot for Surfacing,
taken by Dennis Keeley

You've barely started and the conductor raps his baton on the podium. He looks at you archly.

"You don't know the song?"

"Of course, I've been singing it all my life. But this isn't the one I've learned."

"You've learned the North American version of the song. Obviously. The melody in Italy is completely different."

He looks disgusted with you, rolls his eyes, turns around, and gives some lengthy instructions to someone in Italian.

Someone shoves a sheaf of sheet music at you and sends you back to the hotel. You will have to learn it, get into the key they've chosen, and somehow pull it off without a rehearsal.

Before the concert, you and Dan and the other performers are ushered into the pope's chambers for a private audience. He seems old and frail, with a broken thumb, hobbling on a bad hip. He is surrounded by aides that introduce him to each person he greets. Beside you, Dan, who is Catholic, is practically melting in his shoes. All those years of going to confession are finally paying off.

But you feel awkward and out of place. Once again, you are good. Make a little small talk, don't say what you think about birth control policies, women's issues, gay rights, not to mention the Inquisition and the goddamn Crusades.

You've been told fourteen million people around the world are going to watch the papal Christmas concert on live television.

You are absolutely terrified. You want to stay on key, keep up with the orchestra, do the right thing. Backstage you feel like a wraith, see-through, like smoke. Maybe what happened in Paris wasn't so bad; maybe you just had to kick that hard to make enough space to step through to something new.

You run the lines of the song: *The hopes and fears of all the years are met in thee tonight.* At least when you're onstage tonight, even if laryngitis has you by the throat, the key is out of your natural range, and you may not hit the right note, you will be telling the truth.

If I had a
million

albums

Photographer Al Robb captured Steven Page's "hmm not sure what to call it" dance during a Barenaked Ladies live performance

Those days in the trenches, leading up to Stunt, where Terry did everything he could to put us in the hospital, it really solidified the work ethic of the band. We realized that good things come to those who work themselves to the bone. He also taught us that it's not just work your ass off. It's work your ass off and enjoy it. And be into it.

Ed Robertson, Barenaked Ladies

Barenaked Ladies in San Francisco, photographed by Jay Blakesberg for Stunt promotion

T

he Barenaked Ladies have toured their asses off and they can't get anything going in the United States. They're in the process of recording a third album, *Born on a Pirate Ship*, but they can barely get any airplay in Canada.

It's 1995, they've been together for nearly a decade, and they still feel like a sideshow. They want to be the main act. They're shopping around for new management.

The guy sitting behind the desk tapping away at his computer — the one the Ladies have heard is the best of the best — looks like a teenager. With a toy.

"I think your songs are amazing, and your live show is amazing," Terry says. "You've made an amazing album." He looks up, bright-eyed. "But you guys gotta lose the shorts. We've got to grow up your image."

Ed Robertson says, "This is who we are. People need to look past our shitty shorts and T-shirts and hear the music."

Terry shrugs.

"You guys need to think about this, because you look like fucking dorks," says Terry. "I'm not saying change who you are or lose your sense of humour. I'm saying that if you want people to take you seriously, then you need to present yourselves more seriously."

Then he says exactly what he thinks about the album cover for *Gordon*, their first release. He actually says it's infantile. It's a joke. It looks like it's for kids.

"You don't have to change anything about the way you perform or write music or approach a crowd. You just have to be a little more careful about the way you present yourselves. It's about giving people more opportunity to hear the music. Not less."

There's a refreshing honesty about this guy.

"So, what do you want to do?" Terry asks.

The band explains that they want to go into the studio, get an album out, tour for a couple of months, and then take six months off.

Not only is he honest, Terry seems to have some kind of radar for what's going on between the guys. Some weird intuitive sense.

"You're tired. Your relationships are fucked up, between each other, with your partners back home. One of your guys has dropped out. So here's what I suggest: You take six months off now. Go back home. Steve, Ed, you guys get back to what brought you together in the first place. Start writing again. Because when I get you back, you're going to give me the next two years of your life."

He lays out a plan. It's almost like the words are just coming through him, like the Commandments. He sees it all, right there in the office. "Forget Canada

for now. We're going to go to the US markets, one by one. Then we're going to go to them again. And go to them again. You guys are going to do in-stores, radio stations, meet and greets, after-show meet and greets."

Terry tells them, no ego. Ego kills everything.

"At the end of the day, if you're not happy, or I'm not happy, we walk away and nobody's a dick about it. Okay?"

"Okay."

Two years later, after six months off and eighteen months of touring, they've recorded a live album, *Rock Spectacle*, and put out "Shoebox," an EP, but they're still on the road, their second and third rounds of American markets.

Terry is working "The Old Apartment" as their latest single, and he's working it hard on radio. Wherever there's a spike, they go back to the market to play again. Four performances a day. One full two-hour show a night, six songs in a record store in the afternoon, three songs at a radio station, a meet and greet at night. They're making a stipend of maybe five hundred dollars a week because Terry says he doesn't care about making money for the first two years. It's all about putting money in, putting them

in venues that are bigger, even if there's a smaller return, just to make sure everyone who wants a ticket can get one.

Finally, Ed breaks. The bus has rolled through spectacularly wooded hills into this bucolic lakeside town, but all he can see through the bug-splattered window is yet another diner, yet another all-day breakfast, yet another cup of lukewarm grey coffee. Yet another teary conversation on the phone with his wife, Natalie, who is at home in Ontario with their new baby, Hannah.

He feels uncomfortable in his skin from all the greasy food on the road, puffy and grimy. No matter how much he naps on the bus, he is never refreshed. He and Steven Page, best friends since high school, are barely talking; Ed isn't even reading, that place where he has always been able to lose himself, because he can barely concentrate.

He thinks of Natalie and Hannah. How far away they are, at home in Ontario, how sweet Hannah smells, how she stares at him so matter-of-factly, and presses her soft, pillowy cheek against his. The dimples on her knuckles.

He's already missed one sixth of her life.

He's at the end of his fucking rope. Calls Terry.

"I can't do this. I haven't seen my wife in eight weeks. I could be making more money managing a Wendy's right now. I can't do it anymore."

"Hang in there, guy," says Terry. "Give me three more months. Then we'll have this conversation again."

Ed is almost weeping; he is so exhausted.

"Listen, guy. It's turning. I can feel it. The band is right on the cusp. If a couple more stations fall behind the single, then the momentum will continue to build and you'll break wide open."

Terry has a way of making Ed believe he can keep up the pace.

"I just need you to play for every single American. Then they'll get it."

Terry knows that the Barenaked Ladies' power is not just in their harmonies, but in their personalities. Until now they've just been thinking about albums — but Terry reiterates to Ed this idea that every artist has something that is unique, and it is from that core that the strategy reveals itself.

He's dead right, of course.

When the band gets a few weeks off, they go right into pre-production for their next album, *Stunt*. John Rummen is working on the look of the album, but there are no songs to send him yet.

John has nothing to go on. So he calls and asks how the music feels.

Ed says, "Rebirth."

They are in the studio, hard labour. Terry calls and says, "*Rock Spectacle* has just gone platinum in the US. A million copies."

By the time *Stunt*, with its exquisite expressionistic cover art, is released, the Ladies have barely had time to catch their breath or stop to consider whether or not losing the shorts has really made any difference at all.

They are bussing in to Boston to start it all over again with an in-store at Newbury Comics.

When the in-store is announced, Newbury gets three thousand phone calls.

Andrew Govatsos, the local promoter, says, "We'd better move this outside," and secures City Hall Plaza.

The guys are excited. They think, *Okay, wow. Maybe there will be five thousand people there*. But that would be nuts. That would be beyond expectations.

The bus gets stuck in Boston traffic. "It's weird," says the driver. "The roads are jammed, and it's the middle of the day."

Ed is panicking. "We gotta get there. We're not going to have time to set up. There's probably going to be three thousand people there."

Barenaked Ladies in San Francisco

Barenaked Ladies live during
their "short pants" phase

Ed leans toward the window at the front of the bus, trying to see around the traffic. He notices the car in front of the bus has a Barenaked bumper sticker. Another driver in the next lane over is wearing a Barenaked hat.

They are causing the traffic jam.

By the time their tour bus arrives, there are well over thirty thousand people in the square. By the time they hit the stage, the crowd has reached eighty thousand.

All the work, all the in-stores, all the radio stations. Ed can see now what Terry saw three years before.

It worked. Terry had laid out a plan. He had envisioned the whole thing. Starting with his micro-marketing plan, he had a set of steps required for the band to get there. Everything fell into place exactly as he said it would.

"Now you can wear whatever you want, guys," says Terry.

sarah

rising

*Cathy Barrett, Dan Garnett (tour manager),
Sean Ashby (Sarah's guitar player), Terry,
and Sarah backstage*

The inspiration for Lilith Fair came from Sarah. She threw out an idea that promoters said couldn't succeed. Was it chauvinism? Maybe. The rebelliousness of popular music fit men; men dominated rock radio. In Sarah you had this other voice: universal, spiritual, empathetic, nurturing. Everyone said it would be a commercial disaster. Terry said, "Why not?" The next thing you know, it's become a social movement.

Shaw Saltzberg, Senior Vice-President, Feldman & Associates

Dan Fraser, Sarah, Clive Davis, Terry

t's been eighteen months since the Vatican, and Sarah
doesn't want to go out on the road. Doesn't feel like it.

Fumbling Towards Ecstasy has gone platinum, double, triple, and just keeps on climbing. Sarah's broken big in the US and in Europe.

Terry knows he almost broke her physically, and mentally. But it's almost spring. Summer is coming and he needs to get her out on the road again.

He drops by her place. It's the first home she's ever had that is her own. She bought it. Two years ago she was four hundred thousand dollars in debt.

"No!" she cries out when she sees Terry. She's joking, of course.

Terry laughs. The yard is green and lush.

"Look. Daffodils. Back in Halifax we planted bulbs in the fall. Here, they rot if you do that. I'm putting in the tulips even though it's almost spring. Every colour."

"You're in a bubble. A green bubble."

"I like my bubble." She draws a circle in the air around herself with the trowel. "I'm just as happy painting or making jewellery or gardening. I want to be happy."

She bursts into tears.

Awkward.

"I hate to see anyone cry. Especially a lady."

"Actually, I'm a weeder." She pulls up long, tangled roots that track like a web of rope under the ground.

"Look, it's not what I want. This is your career. It's up to you to derive what you want from it."

One thing he has learned along the way: You can't use force of will to change someone's perspective. It's been trial and error up till now, just trying to keep the artists out on tour. But with Sarah has come a different story. She has an extraordinary reach. He's learned from her by sheltering her, giving her room, pushing her.

"It's like the fog has rolled in," she says. "That fucking Halifax fog. Sorry." She wipes tears away, leaving a streak of earth on her cheek as brown as her eyes.

He hopes she doesn't start talking about her love life. It just makes him uncomfortable. He doesn't mess with her personal life. Doesn't mess with the music.

"You've got to know that my relationship with you is not conditional. Whatever you want. Create your own situation, and I'll be there for you."

Darryl Neudorf, one of the session musicians that Nettwerk brought in to help Sarah on her first album

back when she was green and scattered, has filed a lawsuit claiming he wrote songs for *Touch* and didn't get credited or paid as co-creator.

He waited years, until she finally had some success. Now the guy won't let it go. Won't settle out of court. Worse is the word he's spreading that Sarah's not who she seems to be.

Sarah digs her bare hands into the soggy earth, feels the dirt under her fingernails. Her mother is a gardener; one thing she knows is how weeds can choke the bloom. How deep the roots go, like nerve endings. How you have to get every inch, from underneath, and rip it out.

"Music is part of my life, but it's not my whole life. I want to get my hands dirty. I like it when my hands are dirty."

"You're hiding."

"And?"

There's a fan that came backstage in Ottawa and handed her a white scarf, like some kind of peace offering.

He'd become obsessive, possessive, even filed a lawsuit, claiming her song "Possession" was taken from letters he wrote to her, but admitting he just wanted to get closer to her. Then he killed himself.

Sarah digs where she's cleared the dirt, pushes bulbs in, one after the other.

"I know it's not my fault. But I think about his family. Their loss."

She pushes her hands deep underground, buries a bulb.

"What would it take to get you back out?"

She sits back on her heels, strap of her overalls slipping off her shoulder.

"I don't want to headline. I don't want to carry a tour. I don't want it to be about me."

Terry knows he has to find a way to get Sarah out there that doesn't cannibalize her. She's a marquee artist now. If she's opening it has to be with another big player.

"I got you two dates with Sting, but there's nothing else. So tell me what would excite you."

"Okay. Put me out with another female artist. Paula Cole. She's amazing. We did some dates together. It was fun." She digs her trowel into the earth.

Terry laughs. "It won't work. Radio won't even play two female artists back to back."

Sarah digs deeper. "Then let's put three women together. Four. No, five."

Sarah live at Lilith Fair, 1998

Terry grins. Decides to call her on it. Probably the only way to get her out on the road.

"Why not?"

McBride chooses Pine Knob Amphitheatre in Detroit as the beta test site for Sarah's idea of an all-girl lineup. At best, he thinks, he'll get her out of the dirt and in front of an audience again.

The problem? No promoter will touch the idea.

So Terry calls Sarah's New York agent, Marty Diamond. He gets on board. He's got Patti Smith with a new album, and hell, she's been changing diapers and washing dishes in a Detroit suburb for fifteen years. Throw her in the mix, you'd sell some tickets on curiosity alone.

Dan Fraser, Sarah's long-time tour manager who is now a partner in Nettwerk, isn't so sure.

"Icon, Dan," Marty says. "Smith is an icon. There's gonna be ten babies in that audience named Patti, and it's not because they love the name, it's because an artist influenced them and changed their life."

Dan gets it. Ric gets it. They all do.

No one else does.

The lineup, they are told, is suicidal. Paula Cole, Aimee Mann, Patti Smith, Lisa Loeb, then Sarah to close.

Backstage at Pine Knob, Dan's head is spinning. There's Patti Smith — as worn and familiar and longed for as a leather jacket you gave away years ago — and then there's Lisa Loeb, who's prancing around in some kind of foil miniskirt and go-go boots.

It's like mixing Jack Daniels with crème de menthe. In a snifter. Not a velvet hammer. Worse. A velvet stiletto. To the balls.

The media calls it the Girlie Goddess Tour. The Stripped Tour.

Smith looks a little rough around the edges. Nervous, too, her wiry hair streaked with grey, her features as sharp and bony as Keith Richards on a bad day.

Looks like she's wearing the same pants she had on in 1977 during the Radio Ethiopia Tour, when she flipped off the stage and broke her neck. The rest of what she's got on looks like it came from her dead husband's closet: white shirt, necktie, baggy jacket.

The night is hot and muggy. Patti's in a sweat, wiry filaments of hair glued to her neck, and she hasn't even gone onstage yet.

*Lilith founders: Dan Fraser, Marty Diamond,
Sarah, Terry*

Dan knows she hasn't been on the road in years — and back in the day she played clubs like CBGB, not grassy, tented knolls like Pine Knob. Her teenage son Jackson is here to play with her, and he's as soft and tender as a baby, just fourteen or fifteen. She's been holed up in a suburb for fifteen years doing dishes and writing poetry. Now she's like any other mom, recently widowed. She's back to work.

"Don't be surprised if I cry on the last song. I wrote it for Fred."

That's Fred "Sonic" Smith, her late husband.

Dan feels his protective instincts kick in.

When Smith lifts the hair from the back of her damp neck, shakes her head, lets it fall back into her face, Dan thinks she should try a long braid down the back, like him. You don't even have to wash it, so it works on the road, but hell, he's not going to tell her that. She's a legend.

There's something instinctive Dan does with his voice to calm a nervous performer. He shoots the breeze, and his tone is gentle, like a cradle rocking.

Aimee's set is almost over; the turnaround time with five performers is insane.

"You're probably used to something more rock 'n'

roll. Sarah likes the stage to feel homey. Cozy," he says.

"Sarah likes her little carpets."

He and Smith are standing backstage, watching Aimee Mann finish her set.

"She's got this carpet fetish. They're really important to her. I wrap them up like babies after the show."

He explains how he's in charge of the carpets personally. He could get someone else to do it, but they might not understand.

"She just loves to be barefoot and have her carpets, they make her feel warm and at home onstage," Dan continues, hypnotically. "I'll leave them out there for you, might as well."

Smith looks at him with her big alley cat eyes, like he's a dog. She's wary.

"Some stages have slivers . . . ," Dan explains. "I don't want Sarah to have slivers."

Smith turns her gaze back to the stage. She's had more than her fair share of slivers in her day.

There are fifteen thousand people here tonight. The tickets sold out almost overnight, same for a similar lineup they've got planned for LA, later in the summer. Terry, Marty, Ric, who've all flown in for

the night, are getting excited. They've got an audience; a huge audience. And that's no small feat.

When Smith's moment comes, she walks out onstage and takes the mic, turns her head down, hair shielding her face.

Sarah stands close to Dan and watches from the wings.

Smith launches into "Beneath the Southern Cross." The audience, most of them too young to know her music, is restless as three guitars strum the haunting melody. Smith backs into the song slowly, her voice rich and dark, building with the rhythm, the mournful prayer of it becoming more urgent with every note.

The song ends. Dan can hear the audience chattering, distracted, but Sarah, beside him, quivers with excitement.

Smith struts from side to side, steps back, runs her hands through her hair, and spreads her legs triumphantly. She's a rock star — hard and beautiful and real all at the same time. She pauses, and Dan feels the audience surge. This is a moment, and it's working.

Suddenly, Patti Smith whips her head to the right and horks a huge spitball right on Sarah's favourite carpet.

Dan stops, mid-clap, turns to Sarah, horrified.

But Sarah doesn't care. She has her eyes fixed on Smith, a huge smile on her face. "Fucking awesome!"

Later, in the dressing room, Marty, Dan, Ric, and Terry shake their heads in wonder. It worked. And Sarah is excited again. She's beaming. She's passing out the beer from a box.

"Oh, let's do this again."

Who cares if someone spits on your carpet when you're having that much fun?

Sarah and Ash at Lilith Fair

a star is
born &

branded

In the early days of Avril she could have done Coke and Pepsi — all that stuff. She would have been richer, but I think it would have hurt her. Her reputation was that she was different. It was that difference in her that fans identified with, not just the music.

Terry McBride

Early Avril photo shoot by Kharen Hill

Avril Lavigne and her mom, Judy, have flown into Vancouver to meet with Terry. The sixteen-year-old plunks herself into a chair in Nettwerk's Vancouver office and stares at her sneakers. Strands of long hair fall over her face.

She chews gum and flips her hair around like she'd really rather be at the mall. With her friends.

Anywhere but here. In yet another office.

Arista, in New York, had called Terry. They have this girl from Napanee, Ontario. She's got a power voice, but she's stubborn as hell. Doesn't want to work with the people they've set her up with initially, or sing the songs they've picked for her. Her mom loves Faith Hill, but this kid's gone in a completely different direction. Wants to write her own songs. She's from a town of five thousand, but she's urban. She's no Britney Spears. She's not going to sashay around in a midriff-baring ensemble with a python around her neck.

The girl has floundered a bit, trying to find a sound. Arista finally hooked her up with The Matrix, a powerful songwriting group in LA, and they have an album pretty much done. A great album. Now she needs a new manager.

Terry was on their list. Had he heard of her?

"Have I heard of her?" Terry laughed. "How do you think she got from Napanee to New York?"

He explains: Nearly two years earlier, Mark Jowett had received a videotape showing a fourteen-year-old girl singing karaoke in her parents' basement. The lighting was a bare bulb hanging from a cord, the backdrop was plastic insulation, and the vocals were magic. She sang Sarah McLachlan's "Adia" and "Kiss Me" by Sixpence None the Richer, both difficult songs. She hit the notes, and the whole innocence of it was charming.

Mark Jowett flew to Toronto and arranged to meet Avril at the North by Northeast music conference. The meeting with then-manager Cliff Fabri and her parents went well.

Avril's mom and dad were pleasant, concerned for their kid, but eager to support her. She'd been standing on her bed singing her heart out since she was a toddler and doing the same at church. Mark could see that Avril, who was just fourteen, was really, really shy, at least when she wasn't singing. She drank root beer and played with the dozens of braids she'd twisted all over her head while they hashed out the possibilities.

On the strength of her singing, but not sure if she would be right for Nettwerk, Mark arranged for her to go to New York with Fabri to work with Peter Zizzo, a songwriter and producer signed with the label.

Mark followed a few weeks later and liked what he heard. One night after a session, he took Lavigne,

her parents, Zizzo, and Fabri to grab something to eat at a diner. As evening fell, they walked down Broadway together and stopped in Times Square, mesmerized by the lights, the noise, and the dreamlike blur of yellow cabs, like ribbons in the dark, all going somewhere together.

Shortly after Mark left New York, Fabri invited Arista's A&R rep Ken Krongard down to the studio to hear her. Krongard was so impressed, he invited Arista's new head honcho, Antonio "LA" Reid, to drop by.

When Mark got the call that Arista had put a contract worth, potentially, millions of dollars in front of Avril, he was stunned.

To have another label come in and swoop his artist away after he had laid the groundwork with the demo deal was frustrating. Nettwerk hadn't signed her yet, but they had set up the whole New York trip. They had walked down Broadway together and been dazzled by the same lights.

Mark talked it through with Terry.

Terry said to Mark, "Okay. We take the demo deal and rip it up."

"She has so much potential," Mark argued. "Her voice, her demeanour. Her feel."

"I don't like to get messy. I'm not going to be a hothead. I'm not going to litigate. That's just not interesting to me," said Terry. "Let her go."

Terry didn't even have to weigh it: Start a battle with Arista, with whom they have a pure and positive relationship with their shared clients Sarah McLachlan and Dido? Engage with Cliff Fabri at the expense of a relationship with a major label that's taken years to forge? Nope.

It's not cool to shop an artist that you are already developing with another company. But the way Terry saw it, if that's the way someone was going to do business, he didn't want to do business with them.

It's not that he didn't think Avril was worth fighting for. It's just that he wasn't in grade five anymore. Terry had learned something over the years — it's not worth it to set up a fight in front of the principal's office, even if you're pretty sure he'll intervene.

Now Arista has sent Avril back to Terry, looking for new management. She has never even met Terry. All she knows is that Nettwerk let her go almost as soon as she got to New York, and she's been rocketing through

167

Avril performing during her North American The Best Damn Thing *tour*

the labyrinthine corridors of Arista ever since. She balks at being told what to do. She needs a manager who gets her. And it's not going to be Cliff.

"Why did you drop me?"

It's the first question she asks Terry.

Terry is direct. Tells her the story, reminds her of what was truly at stake. A huge opportunity.

"I knew that Arista could offer you more as a label than we could at that time," he says. "They could offer you a multi-million-dollar recording and publishing deal. This was your dream and I wasn't going to stop you from following that dream. That's why we ripped up our deal. We didn't have to. We did it for you."

She explains that the label wants her to have media training.

"So you'll look people in the eye when you talk," says Terry, nodding.

They want to bring stylists in.

He knows the deal. He remembers Sarah calling from New York after her first encounter with a stylist, saying to him over the phone, "I'm not a fucking baby. I know how to put clothes on myself."

"Just be you," Terry says to Avril. "If it feels right, do it. If it doesn't feel right, don't. You take control of your career by being yourself. Skater punk, mall rat, whatever it is."

When her mom, who is as petite and beautiful as Avril, asks how he would market her, Terry explains.

"Marketing is authenticity. Understanding the artist. Trying to keep them real. A lot of people are pushing them around. Trying to make them be this or that. I don't want her to go out there, media-trained, and be like everyone else.

"I don't care if she stares at her shoes or chews gum. Her audience does that too."

That night the whole gang goes for dinner to Saltaire in West Vancouver to celebrate. Avril leans over to Dan Fraser, all her shyness dropping away, and says, "I want to write my music, my way. I want to be a star."

The album, *Let Go*, sells millions in North America, Australia, and the UK. By the end of the year, Lavigne is the top-selling female solo artist of 2002. She is nominated for five Grammy awards, and around the globe, the nominations and awards keep coming.

In Tokyo, kids chase her down the street, cluster outside her hotel room. She is warmed by the welcome

Avril portrait

Avril and her band celebrate Let Go *going double platinum in Canada*

RIGHT: *Rough drawings of Avril's character for manga comics based on her.*

but also confused. The kids are all wearing neckties. They are copying her. It's not what she wanted.

At first, for Terry, it's all about branding. The plan. "When a marketplace reacts positively, go toward your strengths. You can look at a worldwide marketing plan and try to correct your weaknesses. Or you can look at your strengths and amp those out," Terry says.

Why go to Japan once? Why not work her like a Japanese artist?

She learns to speak a little Japanese. Plays Asia, Singapore, Taiwan, Beijing.

The whole Nettwerk team gets crazily creative — with Avril they find new unions of personality and marketing. Avril and *manga*, Avril and *anime*. It's fun. For everyone.

The thoughts that nag Avril about neckties and authenticity will evaporate in the haze of success. After she moves to LA, Terry sees a change in her — and he recognizes something in himself that is going in another direction, toward home.

dark

angel

Sarah at Lilith Fair, 1998

Sarah's trip to Thailand and Cambodia definitely changed her, and she changed me. Up until Sarah, I can't say that giving back to the community was very high on my agenda. For years it was really hard. Nettwerk was constantly having cash-flow problems, and we were pouring everything back into the company just trying to stay alive.

Now what makes me happy is not just putting out music we love, but what the artists can bring to other people's lives. In my initial conversations with artists, I ask, "What are you going to do when you become a big rock star? What do you care about?"

Terry McBride

Sarah at Lilith Fair, 1998

The sun is already blazing; it's like a knife attack. You have to squint.

Someone slides a pair of Ray-Bans along the table to you. You're here to talk to the reporters, a whole pack of them in Hawaiian shirts, baseball caps, cut-offs, and high-tops or sandals with socks.

The print guys sit cross-legged with dog-eared notebooks in their laps, the radio guys squat down in front with their mics, trying not to block the camera guys. You close your hand over the sunglasses but don't put them on; you want the reporters to see you. You see how many of them have come — more than you anticipated.

Press conferences are hard work and damned annoying. Artists hate them. Always so early in the morning, always the same questions over and over again. But Terry wanted everyone there, and he had given the artists a pep talk beforehand. "We're doing something different here. It's not just about that forty minutes onstage this afternoon. It's about everything else."

Jewel, Tracy Chapman, Paula Cole, and Suzanne Vega — the other headliners who will play today — have all shown up to meet the press.

You put on a cowboy hat, lift your hand to shield the sun.

The press has already dubbed this the Girlie Goddess Tour. What you thought of as a small step — an all-woman touring concert — is apparently a giant leap from the usual guy-hard summer fare of Lollapalooza, Ozzfest, Iggy Pop, and the Warped Tour.

This is a festival named for Lilith, winged demon, dark angel, moon goddess, evil twin, faithless first wife of Adam.

Legend or not, Lilith has always had a bit of an image problem.

For starters, she didn't want to lie under Adam. Hell no.

The story goes something like this: Lilith is drawn from the same earth as Adam. She is no side of ribs.

She stands up, day one, and just as she's dusting the dirt off her knees, before she can even get a good look at the guy, this Jehovah character announces that he's giving her to Adam. Happy birthday.

Without so much as a welcome to the garden of paradise, or a pleased to meet you, Adam wants her to lie under him like a mattress, a blow-up doll.

Okay. Sure. She'll try anything once, but just as she's starting to enjoy herself — throws a leg over and climbs on top — the guy freaks out. Starts ranting and raving like she's the one with the problem.

When Adam gets pushy about it, Lilith pushes back. She had none of the forgivable innocence of Eve.

Sticky note drawings by Sarah

OPPOSITE: *Lilith Fair press conference.*

Lilith didn't fall from the Garden of Eden, she leapt.

She's landed here, in the image on the press packets that already litter the ground around the reporters' feet.

This Lilith is an angelic Venus with the hair of Rapunzel, and beams of light that radiate from her like Guadalupe's halo.

The image came from your doodles, the ones you've been doing for years. Sometimes on paper, in your journals; sometimes at the Nettwerk offices, on John Rummen's desk, the walls, the bottom of someone's shoe. John loved your pen-and-ink drawings of Venus on the half-shell, your lotus flowers and Winged Victories. When you were working together to build an image for the tour, it seemed like Lilith had been there all these years, folded between the pages of your sketchbooks.

Somehow she just came out. She looks softer than her reputation, but who says goddesses don't mellow, don't give themselves to happiness, to transformation?

Nonetheless, "Lilith" still riles the journalists.

A reporter stands up. "Estro-fest, Breast-fest, Vulva-palooza," he smirks. "That's what everyone is calling this."

"That's because Lilith is so damned hard to say," another reporter shouts.

"Why aren't you allowing men on the tour? Do you hate men?" another asks.

You pull your cowboy hat down over your eyes, sit forward, and dig into the ground with the heels of your well-worn Frye boots. "I recently married a man. So no, I don't hate them. And we're getting a puppy once this thing is over. Domestic bliss."

Everyone laughs.

"Besides," you say, "my husband is in the band. So yes, I will have men onstage. And offstage."

"Aren't you worried about catfights backstage?" another reporter asks, his voice heavy with sarcasm. "Someone stealing your favourite lipstick?"

Question number two and you're already picking your way around the lipstick landmines. This isn't a beauty pageant. No one is putting thumbtacks in anyone's stilettos.

You turn and smile at the other women on the panel. "No girl fights, yet."

There is a chorus of titters from the reporters. Cameras click and shutter, a boom dangles over Tracy Chapman's face.

Dan Fraser, standing alongside the press table

with Terry and Marty, winces. Tracy is inordinately sensitive, and Dan knows he'll have to field some distance for her so she feels safe at Lilith.

"This is a friendly, comfortable environment," you tell the reporters, speaking for Tracy and the rest, glancing at them hopefully. "It's how I try to live my life, and it's how I like my world to be."

An awkward silence descends.

"Has anyone read the press packages?" you ask.

Terry holds one up. The reporters flip open the folders with the angelic demon on the cover.

Another awkward silence ensues. It's like they're embarrassed by all this stuff about Lilith refusing to lie beneath Adam, like they're taking the ancient backstory literally.

Finally someone speaks up. "What do you hope to accomplish?"

"We want to have fun. We want to make music with artists we respect. We also want to make this about each community we're playing in. So we're doing a talent search to give new artists a chance to join us, and we are donating a dollar from each ticket sale to a local women's charity."

Terry, who stands with Dan and Marty flanking the press table, gives you a thumbs-up. Marty leans

over and mumbles in his thick New York accent, "I hope we make some money, too." They laugh.

It's a relief to break the tension. You and Terry both get a kick out of Marty. When you all started planning Lilith last summer, Terry had to punt him into the twentieth century. "Listen, Marty, you've got to get on e-mail. That's the only way we can make this thing work." Marty, five-foot-three on tiptoe, was in New York running Little Big Man, his talent agency. Marty said he'd do it for Lilith, but that's it. He was pretty sure that the whole e-mail thing would never catch on.

"E-mail is going to change the world, Marty. You'd better get on board."

"I'm a cherubic little New York Jew. What do I know?"

Cherubic or not, one thing Marty does know for sure is that he's into you. Even back when he was at Arista, you were a passion play — at least that's how he describes it. Now he figures this Lilith thing could be a little cottage industry. Fun. He has no idea that Lilith's dark wings will catapult him and his new agency into the big time, that he will become one of the most respected and well-known agents in North America.

Lilith Fair encore

"Actually," Marty says, leaning over to Terry, "I don't care if we make any money. I just want to be treated like one of the crew. I want a walkie-talkie so I can press the buttons and say, 'What's your twenty?'"

The media scrum continues. "You've got a lot of corporate sponsors," a reporter points out. "How does that mesh with this whole earth-hippie vibe?"

You exchange looks with the other artists. "I'll answer that question, but there are other amazing musicians sitting right next to me. Maybe you want to talk to them about their music, and why they're here, first."

Jewel flashes a gorgeous smile, and the attention turns to her.

Dan is relieved. He wants everyone to feel equally appreciated.

Dan is the one who will sweat backstage, get your little oriental carpets in place, make sure everyone is happy. In years past, he's been on the road with some of the biggest rock bands in the world. He will marvel that there is no hazing at Lilith, none of the macho hierarchy of the Warped Tour, where one rock star supposedly used to shoot the opening acts in the ass with a pellet gun — *Welcome to the road, buddy!*

On this sunny morning at the Gorge, when it all starts, Dan has no way of knowing that he's about to enter a parallel universe, where for three years he will negotiate personalities like an infinite strand of multicoloured beads: Sinéad O'Connor's explosive, edgy energy; Missy Elliott in an air-filled suit that takes longer to inflate than she spends onstage; Christina Aguilera doing three songs to tape (*Uh, who's going to tell her this is about live music?*); Chrissie Hynde of the Pretenders, one tough lady onstage, just likes to have fun backstage; Pat Benatar ripping through a hair-raising version of "Heartbreaker," then having a cry on Dan's shoulder because she misses her kids; Sheryl Crow coming out onstage in flippers and a snorkel when rain drenches the audience in Pittsburgh — true grit.

He doesn't know that by the time this tour has circled North America, Lilith can get any woman she wants. Or that he will have to delicately break it to Prince, that no, he can't have the stage in LA, unless he's backing up Sheryl Crow. No idea the tour will face bomb threats and protests by right-to-lifers stoked by evangelist Jerry Falwell and his followers, the same ones who targeted Teletubby Tinky Winky as a gay role model. They'll decry Lilith Fair as demon worship. It will make headlines across America.

On this day at the Gorge, Dan has no idea that this family of women will seize him by the heart. It'll be a secret he won't want to let out — he's a guy, after all.

Working in the office one day, counting the gate, he will hear the loud, unmistakable voice of Bonnie Raitt, who was number one on the charts that summer, call out, "Who's running this show?"

Jesus Christ. Bonnie Raitt. He knows she's a stoic — what could Lilith have possibly done to upset her? She's been through the worst, coming up when she did through the '70s, being marginalized in the '80s, sweeping the Grammies in the '90s with *Nick of Time*. She's gotta be tough as nails. What has gone wrong? He knows she was anxious about this whole group thing, being around all these people, sharing the stage, how it would all roll out.

In a panic, Dan turns to his wife, Diane, who is working the calculator. As the fair's head bookkeeper, she has been on the tour every step of the way with him, riding the ups and downs of tour management. She just gives him *that look*. He has to go out and face it.

Dan walks out into the hallway, head low, sheepish. Whatever the problem is, he'll fix it.

There, before him, is Bonnie Raitt. Legend. In pink, fuzzy slippers, a housecoat, and curlers.

"I'm the one responsible. I'm the road manager," Dan confesses.

"Well, I just want to say you should be running the fucking UN. This is the best experience I've ever had."

All Dan knows now is that he and Terry and Marty and you have put up everything you all have — heart, soul, money — to get this show on the road, and the all-important first press conference is going sideways.

A guy in a Tilley hat stands up. He wants to know if anyone really thinks people will come to something so blatantly political. So, well, *feminist*. He spits the word out like it's a bad peanut.

Dan gives you that *stay calm* look.

You try to explain that it's not political, not at all. It's music.

People are already arriving, spreading blankets on the lawn of the amphitheatre. There is a hum in the village that will travel with the fair. Merchandise includes artisans and jewellers, as well as traditional T-shirt sales and a Borders tent selling CDs. Bioré is handing out pore strips, and as people walk in, they stick them on their noses like a sign of belonging. Guys, too.

Lilith Fair audience

The corporate sponsor question comes up again. Sure. You had a bit of a hard time with that. On the other hand, it takes a hell of a lot of money to put together a travelling caravan of a show like Lilith Fair. Terry had explained it all. "It's Barnum and Bailey, a three-stage three-ring circus. We need sponsors."

Marty, too. He said, "I want to have people on the lawn feeling like we haven't pickpocketed them. I want the ticket prices to be affordable."

"If we use corporate sponsors, they have to be clean." That was your only stipulation. Well, not your only one.

"We can also have booths for groups that want to educate, but if I don't like what they stand for, they don't get a spot."

Then, between the four of you, another idea emerged: "A dollar from every ticket sold goes directly to a local women's charity wherever we play."

Terry stands up in front of the media, gives a little nod. It's time.

You introduce a woman who is the head of a local domestic-violence charity. The woman is hesitant, but she makes her way to the front. She's not used to the spotlight. Now she's up here in front of the cameras.

She explains that the non-profit she represents is a shelter for women who have experienced domestic abuse and have nowhere else to go. Fundraising is a helluva job; they have volunteers, good people, standing out in front of coffee shops with tin cups, practically. Federal funding has been cut. On a good day, someone will send in a cheque for twenty-five dollars.

The woman notices that everyone is looking at her intently, and suddenly she seems to flutter with shyness.

You hand her a cheque. "From Lilith, to you."

The woman covers her mouth with her hand, gasps for breath, and begins to cry.

The amount of the cheque is close to twenty thousand dollars.

She says she didn't expect this, not at all, at least not this much. And then she is overcome by emotion that is so fucking sincere, so real, it hits everyone present like a wrecking ball.

The woman gathers herself. Looks directly at the reporters, at Terry. "I want to tell you all what this really, truly means."

She takes another moment to compose herself. "It means the difference between closing our doors

Sarah backstage at Lilith Fair

and keeping them open for another six months."

Terry feels shocked by her emotion, like he's a lifeguard again, coming up from the water during a rescue, and he's been holding his breath too long.

All the work of the last year getting this Lilith thing off the ground, the exhaustion, the euphoria, it means nothing compared to this: Seeing someone who is out there on the front lines, getting help from her own community — and knowing just how much it all means to her.

He drifts back to thoughts of his father; how his dad had grown up in poverty, worked the hot, toxic smelters to earn the money for university. How he, Terry, had walked away from what his father sacrificed for and valued most — education — to follow his own path. Ask his father now about his son's success in the music business, and he still replies, "Did Terry tell you about Nettwerk's first ten years?"

Terry remembers Pierre Marchand talking about your songwriting process, how you don't know what you want when you begin, but you recognize it once you're there.

Songs are emotions; Terry has always said that. He's packaged them, shipped them in sealed boxes, promoted them, monetized them. Then this woman steps up and hands it all back to him, out of the box. Right now, right here. For some reason that he doesn't really understand himself, he begins to cry, like he is the one that has just been rescued.

The press conference has turned into a bit of a melee. Suddenly everyone is chattering, excited, and warm. The tension has broken.

Photographers snap the woman's picture, reporters circle her to ask questions and get her story.

You push your cowboy hat back, lean forward, and start to explain a bit about the thought process behind the whole dollar-per-ticket commitment, but no one is listening to you. No one is even looking at you.

They don't need to. This whole damned press conference is about what Lilith can do. Dark angel, mattress girl, brothel girl, Bangkok girl, the one who still floats, starless and supplicant, through your dreams. That girl who dreamed of dreams.

The 1998 Lilith Fair crew

afterglow

cathy:

Having the kids, Mira and Kai, completely changed my life, my priorities. I know Terry was feeling a huge, huge pull. There were so many demands on his time between work and having a family. He had Coldplay at the time and the company was huge, it was exploding. He felt a lot of stress around it.

It was so much of our lives. It was always there, even when we went home and had dinner. There were exciting times, the music, the road — thinking about Lilith, it still gives me chills — and many days when it was just drudgery, long days, tons going on.

Kids changed everything. I couldn't make the commitment the way I had, and that was a good thing.

I will always be inextricably linked to Nettwerk, the music. I'm proud of it, it's in my genes in some way. I'll never get rid of it. Lots of people put their blood, sweat, and tears into Nettwerk and had the same epiphany.

There is life after Nettwerk.

Terry, Cathy, and daughter Mira

THE WHITE HOUSE

WASHINGTON

March 2, 1998

Sarah McLachlan
Nettwork
1250 West Sixth Avenue
Vancouver, British Columbia
V6H1A5

Dear Sarah:

Congratulations on winning two Grammy awards
this year! What a wonderful honor -- and
Hillary and I know how much you deserve it.

We wish you continued great success and
happiness.

Sincerely,

Bill Clinton

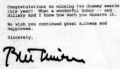

Suisse – Schweiz – Switzerland
Lausanne
Losanna

Hi Terry, Mark, Toni, George, Anna, Irene, Sue, John, Miles, Ric and all I've left out in the ever growing Nettwerk Academy. What do you do if you go to Europe and find out theres no late night food or pizza places STARVE TO DEATH! other than that I'm fine. Hope you're all fine too! looking forward

To seeing you all sometime in the next few years. Yes may not recognise skinny guy 1980's actually thats me now but I'll be skinnier WHATEVER!

NETTWERK PROD.
1717 West 4th st.
VANCOUVER B.C.
CANADA
V6J 1M2

BYE CHOW CHEERS LOVE Tom

Imprimé en Suisse par Orell Füssli SA, Zurich

13031 Edition Photoglob SA, Zürich/VMR

PHOTOGLOB

vinyl

to vinyl

I didn't start with any money; I don't know what I'll end up with. If I can equip my kids with imagination, a sense of self-worth, a conscience, a sense of what's right and what's wrong, I've done my job. I'll be really happy with that. To try and please others? That's all ego. I've got to go down my own path. Do I know the path? No. But I'm pigheaded enough to put on blinders, take a curve or a zigzag, and keep on going.

Terry McBride

Terry at Sarah's charity concert for her music school for inner-city
youth, Ambleside Park, West Vancouver, 2009

F

Picture Terry in lotus position, hands resting lightly on his knees. He's eating raw nuts and drinking coconut water. He's practically wearing a hair shirt. Bliss.

The partners say, "Terry, stop using that fucking lotus position photo for the Nettwerk music material. It's freaking people out."

He just laughs. "Sure. Whatever you want, guys."

He is irritatingly serene about it.

Not only that, but on the one hand he's brokering multi-million-dollar partnerships with Britain's MAMA Group to design entirely new ways of partnering with artists; on the other hand, he wants to tour kirtan artists and release chant CDs on a new label, Nutone. He says he doesn't care if chant makes any money — it makes people feel good. How awesome is that?

He takes the foosball table out of the front room of the Nettwerk offices. "It was getting too competitive," he says. "It wasn't fun anymore."

It's all about the yoga.

The yoga studio — with its cool white walls and bamboo floors, through-the-looking-glass doors and bottomless urn of herbal tea — has become Terry's living room. His new launching pad. And it's a hell of a lot posher than the little living room in Vancouver's west end where he launched Nettwerk, shipped and received, hauled boxes of vinyl up and down the stairs.

Yoga grounds him physically, and when images float through his mind like fish underwater, he watches them and lets them go.

Terry laughs about how annoying he found it when Sarah did yoga, back on the first round of Lilith tours.

"All I knew was that my artist wasn't available to me for ninety minutes of the day," he says. "If I had something to discuss with her, an urgent problem that had to be worked out, too bad. I wasn't allowed to because she was doing yoga.

"I didn't know what yoga was, really, or care. It just irritated me because it was coming between me and something I had to achieve."

Now he's the one with his cellphone turned off because he's working on his Warrior II, his Bridge, his Tree.

Of course, he's not just meditating. Like everything he loves, he invests in it. He monetizes his pleasures. Now, he's opening yoga studios.

Sometimes his partners think his third eye sees too far into the future. What if it leads him astray? What if it never looks back?

Blame it on the tsunami, an elemental collision. Terry, like so many others, was galvanized. Within a week of the Indian Ocean earthquake in 2004, Nettwerk pulled together a lineup — Sarah, Barenaked Ladies, Avril, Sum 41 — for fundraising concerts in Vancouver and Calgary. No one said no.

At the after-party, Terry meets Lara, a yoga teacher. Laying the charm on thick, he explains that he's taken a yoga class or two because, well, he and his wife, Cathy, have split. The girls at the office have advised him that if he wants to meet women, yoga classes are the place.

Lara doesn't sign on for dating, but she does sign on to teach yoga at Nettwerk. She comes in every day and unrolls her mat. Terry takes on a thirty-day challenge — it's intense, it whips him. So he keeps at it. Next he tries a forty-day challenge. Before he knows it, like music, yoga carries him away.

For the first year or two, it's purely physical. It takes him a long time to understand that it's also mental. For those ninety minutes, he hardly thinks of anything else. Thoughts come and go, but his mind is quiet.

He likes it. He doesn't have to win.

It brings him back to some place he remembers, like a song.

Yoga starts as one thing and becomes another. First a problem, then a solution. Like Sarah, who kept him waiting in the bus just long enough to get him interested, although she'd say that she just wanted to finish her pinball game. Like Lilith. All he wanted was to get Sarah touring, to support her album.

She threw it out there. Doesn't want to headline.

Wants a back-to-back all-chick lineup. Not only that, she wants tables for charities. Terry thinks about how all of a sudden he has to deal with fucking charities tabling at his event, which is yet another production issue. It's a pain in the ass.

He has to pile it on his production manager, his tour manager: the e-mails, the people, the booths, the stuff to auction. But he can't think of any reason why not to do it.

Only later is he able to step back and see that it was Lilith that opened him up in some way, taught him something. Changed him.

Lilith snowballed into a pop culture phenomenon, earning a place on the cover of *Time* and *Rolling Stone*, and, after three years, raising over ten million dollars for North American charities that benefit women. And it wasn't because of him, or Nettwerk. It was because of the people who came to hear the music.

At the final Lilith show, on the third and final tour, it rains. They are in Alberta, at Commonwealth Stadium. The rain on the field is slow, a cold, depressing pour, water shushing over any remaining embers in the fire. Sarah is sick. It's tough to load in, tough to load out. At 3 a.m., Dan, Cathy, Terry, and Sarah and her husband

Terry with Ash Koley

Ash stand by the bus in the mournful, empty parking lot. Happy it's over, sad it's over, mad it kept going for so long, afraid that returning to their lives will be like opening a trunk left behind. Will moths fly out? Pandora's creatures? Some snake coiled around a piece of forgotten fruit?

Will there be a chance to do anything like this again? To change the business? Because it's there, where the needle hits the wax and changes the air with just a vibration — that feels good, like acceleration on a curve.

They don't speak; they are exhausted from lack of sleep, cold from the rain, and gutted.

When they get to Vancouver, dry-eyed from restless sleep, each hair on their skin crystallized with salt and sweat, their hair smelling of the musty air conditioner of the bus, it's *See you later. Bye. We'll talk. All right.*

It will be all right.

Sarah and Ash settle down, have two daughters, and, just as quickly, divorce; Terry and Cathy also have two children, and also divorce.

Halfway through Sarah's first pregnancy, her mother dies.

She buries her mother's ashes in her own garden, under a rose bush that resists all fungus and black spot. It blooms relentlessly under her care, sheds handfuls of petals in lavender and pink.

Among the Nettwerk family, each will have minefields to negotiate.

Their children will roll their eyes, prefer the music of Lady Gaga, clamour to watch TV, refuse to do their homework or go to bed, and are not really that interested in what their parents have accomplished. This will bring sanity, sweetness, and humility — the relief and chaos of ordinary life.

Just as CDs replaced vinyl, digital downloads will replace CDs, artists become more independent and labels less important.

Terry will use his Teflon resilience like a superhero, deflecting every loss — Avril, Coldplay, Barenaked Ladies, partners, friends, employees — nothing matters as much as what might yet be.

Somewhere in there, Terry will understand that he is not happy. It really is that simple. The business, like university so many years before, leaves him no time to breathe. He wants to breathe. He has always joked, "I'm one of the most powerful men in the music industry, but I can't carry a tune."

Terry in his office

When he can breathe, he can speak. Then, the road is wide open. Yoga makes him feel abundant. Happy. In tune.

He has only ever invested time and passion and money in things that resonated within. Really good music that he loves.

"Doesn't that sound like yoga?" he says.

Where will the music industry go?

He doesn't know, but he's curious. He's got a pretty good idea that a whole group of kids coming up in the digital age will tell the industry everything it needs to know through their behaviour alone.

He will continue to try and explain what he senses, but what no one else seems to get: A song isn't about ownership. A song is an emotion. A bookmark in your life. Music sees what you cannot, and remembers what you will not. Where you were when you heard it, how the air smelled, how the skin of the body next to yours felt, how the moment tasted, how the moon through the curtains floated like a bright possibility. Every time you hear that song, you feel it, like it's part of you. You want others to feel it too.

He tells his partner Dan that he is a futurist.

That's all fine, Dan thinks to himself — *I'm a realist.*

What about the business? They've got to get this show on the road. Physical isn't selling; vinyl is coming back, if only as a novelty. A song on the road, person-to-person, that's what will keep it all going.

Terry talks about pulling music from the clouds. When artists make music, fans collaborate. There are no new songs. There is only what we bring to each song that makes it unique.

Downloads? It's cultural democracy. The challenge is to figure it out, get your balance, and ride it like a wave, even if everyone else is still waiting for a better one to break behind you.

Staying afloat in the daylight is all about knowing when to shift with the current.

In the summer of 2010, Lilith will struggle to find her wings as recession strikes summer concert goers in the pocketbook. But her sound will remain the same: a call, a song. Terry will ask, how do we transform?

When he is home at night, in his bedroom, Terry will carefully open the smoked Plexiglas cover of his record player — the same one he had when he was a teenager. In the dark, he will slip a record from its jacket, palm it expertly by its grooved sides, and drop the needle down.

He still just loves the sound.

rio Q&A

talking with ric arboit

Nettwerk Founding Partner & President of Nettwerk Productions

Why Nettwerk?

When Terry offered me a partnership, I said, "Why me?"

He said, "We get along."

For a long time at the office, I had worked on a volunteer basis. I only got paid when I was on the road with a band. I never expected to become a partner, but it just felt right.

It was pretty organic. I never thought, *I'm going to my job*. It just felt like, *I'm waking up and I'm doing what I love.*

Why Terry?

Early on I recognized some brilliance in Terry. He had the ability to instill a drive in people. It sparked something in me.

What does it mean to be a label now?

That's what I can't tell you. A label invests in talent and support and day-to-day living so the artist can produce the music. The music business has changed, and it's still changing. Retail has shrunk.

Used to be I'd come into the office, and the first thing I did was look at the ships. What did we ship out? It was all physical. Now I look at iTunes.

The moment the first MP3 showed up online,

and Napster came to an end, you couldn't stop it. I thought, *There's got to be a way to get back to vinyl*. Because you can't share vinyl. To me it was obvious. In 2001, Apple came out with a slogan: Rip, Mix, Burn. The software was there — someone buys a CD, you copy it, burn it to a blank. Right then I knew there was a problem. Now it's gone further than that.

We're all music fans first. We're talking about music. We're all on different boards. I was on the CIRPA board, the FACTOR board. The conversations were coming up, the fears. There isn't going to be enough R&D money finding new artists, developing them. It's expensive. That's where I get my fun and joy — finding something I really, really love

I didn't want people to steal music. I didn't want to throw them in jail, either. It's a drag.

Terry's thing was, don't sue the music fan. What other business is going to survive by suing its customer? It doesn't make sense.

Terry was out there early, restructuring for a digital business model and arguing within the industry to support and go with the change.

He took a stand and we're still paying for the blowback. We got e-mails from our business partners saying, "You can't do that." Everyone had locks on

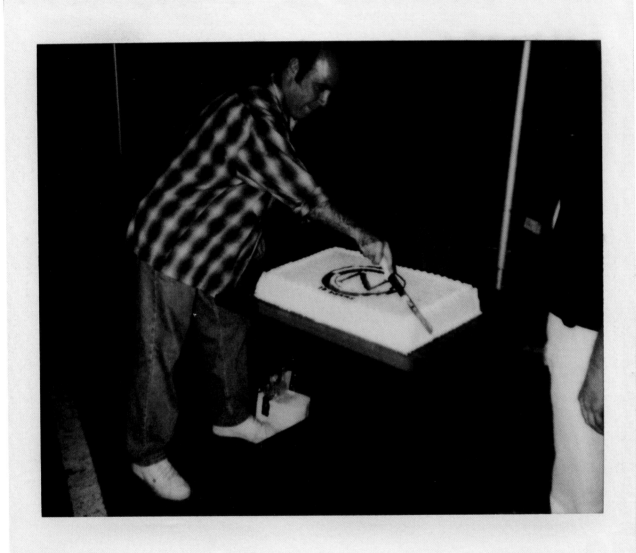

their MP3s. We were pretty much the first company ever to not have locks.

They said, "This is against corporate policy."

We said, "It's not against our policy."

A locked master is music you've bought from your online store of choice. You can put it on your iPod. But if you have another computer, or a friend, you can't transfer it, or burn it onto a disc to play in your car.

We started releasing MP3s that had no locks on them. The company that was distributing us had a policy: We don't do that. Our point of view was it's better for our music at our level to find its way to as many people as possible. To us, it's no different than in the old days, sending out promo copies to three thousand people. Instead, we're now going to give it to you for free.

Terry stepped up. As early as 2003, he was speaking at all these conferences, saying this is the future. Let's go with it. I used to take the flak.

Thanks, Terry, you did it again.

Ric cutting Nettwerk's 10th anniversary cake,
West 6th Street office, Vancouver, 1994

Ric, Dan, Terry, and Mark fishing in the Queen Charlotte Islands

The music business was historically a top-down hit-making machine. The young music entrepreneurs of the '60s — people like Clive Davis, Berry Gordy, David Geffen — knew how to capitalize on the shared social values of the boomers' youth movement and turn it into gold. Record companies, local radio, and national TV eventually became aligned.

The entrepreneurs manipulated radio for decades, paying and taking payola, jamming hits; it became a decadent spiral . . . eventually what charted on *Billboard* was not real. The arc from social activism to decadence was twenty-five to thirty years.

Then comes the technological age. Someone invents SoundScan and SoundScan invents Terry. Terry was one of the first managers to use sales data in a scientific way.

Terry had a scrappy indie company, based in Vancouver, Canada — not exactly the centre of the music business — which was not influenced by historical forces or any of the big guns of the industry. Terry didn't have much money, but he had major ambition and a new methodology. He was a data hound and began using new technology the minute it arrived. It allowed him to look at things from thirty thousand feet, but to apply what he learned at a grassroots level.

I remember booking Sarah McLachlan into a five-hundred-seat venue in Saskatoon in the early days. Sarah had never been to the market before. No promoter would make an offer, so I advised him to skip the city altogether. Terry told me not to worry, that she would sell out the theatre. He knew the SoundScan and radio data in a market where I had no ticket sales history.

He told me to get a promoter and we'd play without a financial guarantee, just a percentage of the profit. We sold out. He used research to micro-market his artists this way until he had a national story.

Shaw Saltzberg

terry
Q&A

Terry in his office

brave new world

A Conversation with Terry McBride about The Digital Revolution

You have been called a visionary. Because of your ability to key in to new technologies, it's like you can see the future in some mystical way.

"Visionary" is not a word I apply to us. We were just a bunch of young kids who were looking forward and having fun. We were techies. I remember showing Clive Davis and Roy Lott at Arista a QuickTime movie. Clive said this would never work. It's absolutely funny to think about it now. Back in the '80s, in two years you would have seen no change at all in the [music] industry. Now, it's changing every minute.

When was the first great sea change?

The introduction of the CD, which did two things: First, it opened up the digital files because they were unprotected.

Second, it introduced what was probably the most profound behavioural shift in young consumers. For the first time, you could hear the same song over and over again without having to move a needle or rewind that tape.

The eight-track was the closest thing to it, but that lost out. But with the CD, as anyone with a kid knows, if you have to play the same song over and over

again to avoid a meltdown in the back seat while you're driving, that's exactly what you're going to do.

How did that translate to the consumer?

We suddenly went from a society that pushed music — pushed how you heard it, when you heard it, where you bought it, and at what price — to one where you could hear music when, how, and as often as you wanted. To me it was the beginning of a huge shift. I only knew music from having it pushed at me. The millennium generation, those kids born 1984 and forward, got used to being able to pull music.

When you were that kid working at Odyssey Imports, didn't you "pull" music by choosing imports and alternative releases over *Billboard*'s Top 40? The record store was a hangout where you shared music, peer to peer. How was that different than online music sharing?

I still had to go get it. I had to go buy it. I'm buying it where I'm told to buy it, at a price I'm told to pay.

The advent of pulling music was, literally, you didn't have to buy it. It happened with everything, from music to file sharing to Netflix. Anything that used to be pushed could now be pulled.

Through it all, music was becoming more and more popular. Where ten years earlier you hardly heard any music in movies other than the score, now you would hear songs. Everything was shifting. My point of view was that the CD was the problem, but not because of why you might think it was. The unlocked files on the CD allowed the shift in behaviour from push to pull. The minute that happened, you lost control of the copyright. My idea was if you wanted to monetize the business, you had to monetize the behaviour of the consumer.

You responded counter-intuitively.
No, it was intuitive. Everything I've done has been intuitive.

When all the debate was going on about file sharing, the initial industry reaction was fuck 'em, sue 'em, bury 'em, and all that sort of stuff. I got that, loud and strong. Then I went, *Okay, what else is there?* Harvard Business School had released a study on the impact of file-sharing on CD sales, so I read it. Pew Research had also released studies. So I started reading those, too, and it was really a different point of view. It was a point of view purely based on facts. The Harvard data showed that, although the RIAA still believed downloads were killing CD sales, other market factors were at work, and downloads were not the only thing displacing CD sales.

It got me thinking more, *Okay, file sharing is here. It's not going to go away*. You can fight it, but ultimately, you're going to lose. So I started asking, *Where does Nettwerk go?*

I started to listen to the music fans. I'd go online and talk with them and read what they were talking about, try to get an essence of where they were coming from, try to put myself where I was when I was their age. I started to look at the behaviour.

The behavioural shift was no different from what any other teenagers had ever done. Kids have always shared music. This time it was based on the use of technology.

Back in the day, a kid would buy an album, tape it for the car, or take it to a friend's house, and make a mixed tape.
Right. And the business has always had an issue with that.

There was a blank-tape levy in Canada for many years, and that was the music business trying to say, *The only reason someone's going to buy a blank cassette tape is to record one of our albums to give to one of their friends.* In Japan there were levies on CD rentals.

With the advent of Napster, the labels became really, really fearful.

You weren't fearful, you were curious?
Over some frigging Christmas holiday, I said, "Okay, if it's the behaviour, why is it the behaviour?"

I remember reading a psychology article that said the imprinting of your subconscious gets stronger with every sense that's associated to it, so if you can combine smell with taste, the chance you'll remember something goes up.

So that made me think about how songs that have videos usually sell more, because now there are two things: visual and aural. But they really sell if they touch a chord in someone's emotion. Songs aren't products. They are emotions.

For example, we'd done four singles from *Surfacing*, Sarah's fourth album, but hadn't gotten to "Angel" yet, because Arista says it's not a single. So we place it in the movie *City of Angels* during the love scene.

The *City of Angels* soundtrack has two singles — one by the Goo Goo Dolls and one by Alanis Morissette. Now, Sarah's own label won't release "Angel," but Warner Brothers wants it to be the third single off the soundtrack. So I said, "Okay. You guys work 'Angel.'" Now Warner Brothers is working "Angel" rather than Sarah's own record label.

About halfway through the process, Arista jumped in and helped. I knew the minute that song was played on a radio station, the phones would start to ring. Sarah was at the top of her game. That was a massive movie. People would instantly react to that song because of the emotional quality — plus it was attached to an emotional scene in a movie.

That really nailed for me the concept of the song as an emotion. Just putting a song in a TV show or movie helps, but if you can create an emotional attachment to it, then you've got that psychological double. It's not just hearing it. It's visual; it's relational. So that's the whole process of me coming to that concept of songs as emotions.

The missing piece is, when you first heard "Angel," you must have connected with it emotionally, without the help of that supporting sensory element.

From day one, I knew "Angel" was a hit. Sarah had a neat habit of not wanting to play me anything new until she was really, really happy with it. But somewhere on tour she decided to play "Angel" for me at a radio station, because she really loved it. I managed to get a tape of it so I could actually hear it. When I can listen to a song three or four times and a couple of days later find myself humming it, it's got me. Subconsciously it's got me. "Angel" had me.

During this whole moment of change, you supported file downloaders against lawsuits.

One. It was a family down in Texas. A fifteen-year-old girl, Elisa Greubel, came to our attention because she had e-mailed one of our artists, MC Lars, to say that she identified with his tune "Download This Song" because her dad was being sued for downloading music.

She had file-shared Lars's music off her family's computer, as well as Avril's "Sk8er Boi." So her dad, David, was one of thousands of seemingly randomly targeted downloaders to be sued by the Recording Industry Association of America.

I decided to put up the money to defend this case because my artists would never sue a fan. None of them. So when the major labels who technically own the copyrights or the RIAA sue, it's like the artist is suing. Well, the artist is not suing.

Suing the consumer is wrong. You cannot win by fear, by trying to make people afraid. Suing your customer is not a winning formula.

The bottom line is out of all these lawsuits — which they were settling for five thousand dollars here, ten thousand dollars there — the lawyers were collecting all the money. There was nothing going back to the artists, the publishers, or the music labels. It was a campaign of fear.

The pain of litigation was destructive to our music business. It was hard for me to stand by and say, "This is a good thing." I was a member of the RIAA.

I went and spoke to them. I told them that I couldn't stand by. This is so wrong. I'm going to defend one downloader; I'm going to make it a really big issue. And if we lose, we'll play a benefit concert, and you're going to lose the PR battle. This has to stop. You're killing the business.

It was a really conscious decision on your part.

Yes. It wasn't about winning a copyright case. It was about saying, "This approach is wrong, and it won't work."

What was the reaction from the people closest to you at Nettwerk, your partners?

Lukewarm. Some of my producers were quite upset, because they have to work with the major labels, and I was taking a stand that was contrary to where the major labels were. All the major labels would moan in their ears, "You're working for a bunch of idiots," and "How dare they do this."

Back then, it was not a very popular thing. Not within the business. It created a whole controversy.

I remember the fear. We were all saying, "We'd better stop downloading and sharing. They're going to track us on the computer and find us." Big label equals Big Brother.

What does that do? It makes the consumer think the artists are just fat cats. The music business is just a bunch of corporate suits. They've always mistreated the artists, so it became about no respect. There was no respect for what the artist was doing. It was completely counter-intuitive.

Did you meet the Greubel family?

I never met the family, but I spoke to them a number of times, and I spoke to the lawyer a number of times. We fought the case for three years. Ultimately, it settled for basically nothing.

By the time it settled, the RIAA had stopped suing. They had realized they could not bring down peer-to-peer file sharing. You can't use litigation to change the behaviour of the public; it just won't work. What will work is to understand what the behaviour is, and then to create value around that behaviour, and monetize it that way. That's what the music business did not want to do. It's happening now.

Was it easier for you to be forward-thinking in the digital marketplace because, compared to some of the major players, you're relatively small?

Absolutely. But also, almost everything that Nettwerk has done has been a bit different. We were that company that, you know, created the enhanced CD, no one else was doing it. We're the company that created Lilith. We've always done things differently. We've always done it from our point of view. That's not to say that everybody else was doing it wrong. We just have our own way.

A continuation of the various Nettwerk artists over the years

25 YEARS OF NETTWERK ARTISTS

ABIGAIL WASHBURN • A CAMP • ACTUAL TIGERS • ADRIENNE PIERCE • ALEXI MURDOCH • ALEX LLOYD • ALIQUA • ALPHA • AMY CORREIA • ANATHALLO • ANDY HUNTER • ANGUS & JULIA STONE • ASH KOLEY • AUTOUR DE LUCIE • AVIA • AVRIL LAVIGNE • BAD BOY BILL • BADMARSH & SHRI • BARENAKED LADIES • BEAM VS CYRUS • BE GOOD TANYAS • BEL CANTO • BERTINE • BHAGAVAN DAS • BILLY TALENT • BLAKE CARRINGTON • BOMBAY BICYCLE CLUB • BOXCAR • BRAINBOX • BRANCACCIO & AISHER • BRAND NEW • BROTHERS AND SYSTEMS • BT • BUTTERFLY BOUCHER • BUZZCOCKS • BY DIVINE RIGHT • CALM • CASINO • CHANTAL KREVIAZUK • CHILDMAN • CHRIS & COSEY • CHRISTINE EVANS • CINDERPOP • CLUMSY LOVERS • COLDPLAY • CONJURE ONE • CONSOLIDATED • CORALIE CLÉMENT • DATAROCK • DAVID BRIDIE • DAVID GRAY • DAVID MEAD • DAVID NEWMAN • DAVID USHER • DAYNA MANNING • DELERIUM • DEPARTURE LOUNGE • DIDO • DIESELBOY • DJ COLETTE • DJ DAN • DONNA DE LORY • DOWNLOAD • DUSTED • ELLEGARDEN • ELSIANE • ERIN MCKEOWN • EVOLUTION • FALLING JOYS • FAUXLIAGE • FC KAHUNA • FEAR OF MUSIC • FELIX DA HOUSECAT • FERRABY LIONHEART • FINAL CUT • FINN BROTHERS • FIVE FOR FIGHTING • FLANNEL JIMMY • FOGHORN STRINGBAND • FRAZEY FORD • FRONT 242 • FUN • FUSSIBLE • GABRIEL & DRESDEN • GILL LANDRY • GINGER • GOB • GREAT LAKE SWIMMERS • GRIFFIN HOUSE • GUSTER • HADOUKEN! • HALOU • HANNE HUKKELBERG • HEM • HILT • HOPE SANDOVAL • HOWLING BELLS • HYBRID • ITCH • IVY • IZDATSO • JACK HARLAN • JAI UTTAL • JAMES YUILL • JARS OF CLAY • JAY BRANNAN • JAZZ UPSTARTS • JENIFER MCLAREN • JENNY OWEN YOUNGS • JESCA HOOP • JET SET SATELLITE • JOE PISAPIA • JOHN MANN • JOHNNY FOREIGNER • JOSH ROUSE • JUNIOR JACK • JUNKIE XL • K-OS • KAMERA • KARIN STRÖM • KATHRYN WILLIAMS AND NEILL MACCOLL • KATZENJAMMER • KELLY JONES • KENDALL PAYNE • KEVIN HEARN • KIDSTREET • KINKY • KIRSTY HAWKSHAW • KREC • KRISHNA DAS • KRISTY THIRSK • KYLE ANDREWS • LADY OF THE SUNSHINE • LADYTRON • LAVA HAY • LEIGH NASH • LESTER • LHASA • LILI HAYDN • LILY FROST • LISA GERRARD • LISSIE • LUCE • LUNIK • MADREDEUS • MANDO DIAO • MANUFACTURE • MARC MOULIN • MAREN ORD • MARGARET

CHO • MARIA TAYLOR • MARTHA WAINWRIGHT • MARTINA SORBARA • MARTIN LEDUC BAND • MARYKATE O'NEIL • MATT & KIM • MATT WERTZ • MC 900 FT. JESUS • MC LARS • MEDIAEVAL BAEBES • MELISSA MCCLELLAND • MEN WOMEN & CHILDREN • MIRANDA LEE RICHARDS • MOEV • MOIST • MOKA ONLY • MOLLY JENSON • MORGAN PAGE • MOUTH MUSIC • MYSTERY MACHINE • NATARAJ • NATHAN • NEIL FINN • NNEKA • NOEL SANGER • NORTEC COLLECTIVE • OH SUSANNA • OLD CROW MEDICINE SHOW • ORGANIC AUDIO • PANURGE • PAPA BRITTLE • PAPER MOON • PAR-T-ONE • PAUL VAN DYK • PEACE/LOVE & PITBULLS • PEZZ • PLUMP DJS • PO' GIRL • POVI • P.O.W.E.R. • PRETTY GREEN • RAINE MAIDA • RAVEN MAIZE • RAVERS ON DOPE • REEMA DATTA • RIO KLEIN • ROBERT POST • RON SEXSMITH • ROSE CHRONICLES • ROSIE THOMAS • SANDBOX • SANDRINE • SARA LOV • SARAH MCLACHLAN • SARA MELSON • SATELLITE CITY • SEAFOOD • SEAN JOHNSON • SEAN MACDONALD • SENSE FIELD • SEVERED HEADS • SHAWN HLOOKOFF • SHELLEY CAMPBELL • SHE'S SPANISH, I'M AMERICAN • SHIRLEY BASSEY • SINGLE GUN THEORY • SIXPENCE NONE THE RICHER • SKINNY PUPPY • SMOOTHER • SOUNDS FROM THE GROUND • SPK • STATE RADIO • STEREOPHONICS • STEVEN PAGE • ST. LOLA IN THE FIELDS • STYROFOAM • SULLY • SUM 41 • SUZANNE LITTLE • SWOLLEN MEMBERS • TARA MACLEAN • TARRENTELLA • TASTE OF JOY • TEKLA • TELEFUZZ • TERRIBLY EMPTY POCKETS • THE ALEXANDRIA QUARTET • THE AQUANETTAS • THE BROTHERS CREEGAN • THE CARDIGANS • THE DEVLINS • THE DIVINE COMEDY • THE FORMAT • THE GRAPES OF WRATH • THE GRASSY KNOLL • THE GRUESOME TWOSOME • THE HACKENSAW BOYS • THE HAMPDENS • THE HERMIT • THE HUNDREDS AND THOUSANDS • THE IDS • THE LEEVEES • THE PERISHERS • THE PINKER TONES • THE PROCLAIMERS • THE RIFLES • THE RIVER PHOENIX • THE SCUMFROG VS. BOWIE • THE SUBMARINES • THE TEAR GARDEN • THE VERBRILLI SOUND • THE WATER WALK • THE WEEPIES • THE ZAMBONIS • TIËSTO • TOBY LIGHTMAN • TOM ALLALONE & THE 78s • TOM MCRAE • TOM THIRD • TREBLE CHARGER • TRESPASSERS WILLIAM • TRISCO • UH HUH HER • UTAH SAINTS • VENUS HUM • WADE IMRE MORISSETTE • WAH! • WAY OUT WEST • WEED • WILD STRAWBERRIES • YOUNG DRE THE TRUTH

random nettfacts

- Nettwerk's birthday is the same day as co-founder Mark Jowett's son, Paul.

- Original Moev singer Madeleine Morris's mother wrote the original "Hockey Night in Canada" theme song. If you don't know this song then you are obviously not from Canada (ask any Canadian to sing it — they will).

- Mark Jowett used to play in a heavy metal band called FOXX in high school, and he played bass in E, one of Vancouver's first electronic bands.

- Delerium co-founder Bill Leeb was once a member of Skinny Puppy.

- Delerium co-founders Bill Leeb and Rhys Fulber are also the co-founders of industrial group Front Line Assembly.

- Sarah McLachlan's biggest hit in Europe was actually a Delerium track that she co-wrote and sang ("Silence").

- Sarah McLachlan's biggest single to date in North America is "Angel" (#1 on *Billboard*'s singles chart).

- "Angel" is used in the ASPCA commercial that Sarah filmed.

- Sarah funds an outreach program in Vancouver that provides music education for inner-city children.

- Highest number on the *Billboard* chart for a Sarah album: #2

- Highest-charting single for Barenaked Ladies: "One Week." It reached #1 on the singles chart.

233

- Biggest-selling Barenaked Ladies album to date: *Stunt*

- At one point there were seven Catherines, all with different spellings, working in the Nettwerk office. They became known as the K/Catherii (as named by Chris Hooper of The Grapes of Wrath).

- Avril Lavigne was 17 when she signed to Nettwerk (management).

- Sarah McLachlan was 18.

- Number of songs Sarah had written when she was signed: 0

- Nettwerk's design group, Artwerks, has been nominated for 8 Junos and has won 2.

- Sarah McLachlan has been nominated for 21 Junos and has won 8.

- She has been nominated for 7 Grammys and won 3.

- Barenaked Ladies were nominated twice for a Grammy.

- Nettwerk had a clothing line for five years called Chulo Pony.

- Avril has a clothing line called Abbey Dawn.

- Avril's biggest single to date: "Girlfriend"

- Avril's biggest-selling album: *Let Go*

- Nettwerk had a book publishing company called Madrigal Press.

- Madrigal Press released an authorized biography of Barenaked Ladies written by Paul Myers (brother of actor Mike Myers).

- The two women of Nettwerk band Lava Hay each married someone from Nettwerk band The Grapes of Wrath.

- Then-Nettwerk artist Avril Lavigne married then-Nettwerk-managed band Sum 41's Deryck Whibley.

- Both Terry McBride and Mark Jowett dropped out of UBC to focus on Nettwerk.

- Nettwerk artist Griffin House turned down a golf scholarship to play music.

- Tara MacLean was first discovered by Nettwerk when she was singing on a BC Ferry.

- Old Crow Medicine Show was first discovered by Doc Watson's daughter while they were busking outside a pharmacy.

- The Be Good Tanyas first played together at tree-planting camps in remote British Columbia.

- Early Nettwerk artist SPK (Graeme Revell) once recorded a complete album using only the sounds of insects.

- MC 900 Ft. Jesus song "The City Sleeps," which explores the mind of a serial arsonist, was banned from a US radio station.

- Sarah made the cover of *Time* magazine for her work with Lilith Fair. The headline read "The Gals Take Over."

- In 1998, Lilith Fair was the top-grossing festival in the world.

- Number of Lilith Fair shows between 1997 and 1999: 139

- Chantal Kreviazuk has written songs for/with Avril Lavigne, Kelly Clarkson, Hilary Duff, Mandy Moore, Gwen Stefani, and Carrie Underwood.

- Blake Hazard of The Submarines is the great-granddaughter of famed novelist F. Scott Fitzgerald.

- Lilith Fair grossed over US$10 million for charity.

- Dido was born on Christmas Day, so she also celebrates an official birthday on June 25th, following the example of Paddington Bear.

- Dido's full name is Florian Cloud de Bounevialle Armstrong.

- Abigail Washburn was Colorado College's first East Asian studies major.

- Leslie Fiest was a member of the Nettwerk band By Divine Right alongside Brendan Canning, who is now in Broken Social Scene.

- Nettwerk has had six different locations in Vancouver:
  1) Terry's apartment
  2) a one-room office in an office building on Granville Street in Vancouver
  3) a big one-room office on Homer Street in Vancouver
  4) the first floor of a retail space on 4th Avenue
  5) next door to Mushroom Studios in Vancouver
  6) its present space, on West 2nd Avenue, Vancouver . . .

- Nobody in The Grapes of Wrath had read the book when they named the band.

- Ladytron is named after a Roxy Music song.

- MC 900 Ft. Jesus's name came from an Oral Roberts sermon in which the evangelist claimed that he had received a vision of a 900-foot-tall Jesus who commanded him to build a hospital.

- Singer-songwriter Rosie Thomas also performs as a stand-up comedian under the name Sheila Saputo.

- Kinky's song "We Are the Galaxy" is the official anthem for the LA Galaxy Major League Soccer Club.

- Terry was on the Olympic Canadian Field Hockey Team. He would also probably have been on the Olympic Foosball team if there was one.

INDEX

A

Abbey Dawn (clothing line), 234
"Addiction" (Skinny Puppy), 59
"Adia" (McLaughlin), 165
Aerosmith, 98
Aguilera, Christina, 185
AIDS, 51
American Society for the Prevention of Cruelty to Animals
    (ASPCA),
"Angel" (McLaughlin), 225, 226, 232
Apple, 213
Arboit, Dan, 53
Arboit, Ric, 49, 53–54, 57, 101, 152, 155–56, 213, 215
Arboit, Tarcisio (Terry), 54
Arista, 97–98, 119, 165, 167, 170, 183, 223, 225
Artwerks, 234
Asian brothels, 111
Australia, 170

B

Bacharach, Burt, 51
Baez, Joan, 79
Bangkok, 111
Barenaked Ladies
    biggest-selling album, 234
    fundraising concerts, 203
    Grammy nominations, 234
    highest-charting single, 232
image, 137, 140
leaves Nettwerk, 207
relationships within band, 137, 139
    tours, 139–40
    work ethic, 135
Barrett McBride, Cathy, 35, 38–43, 194, 204, 207
Barrett McBride, Kai, 194
Barrett McBride, Mira, 194
Battle of the Bands (Vancouver Province & UBC), 33
Bayer Sager, Carole, 51
Be Good Tanyas, The, 235

Beatles, 53
Beijing, 173
Benatar, Pat, 185
"Beneath the Southern Cross," 156
"Ben's Song" (McLaughlin), 82, 85
Bhopal (India), 51
Biafra, Jello, 53
Billboard, 119, 218, 232
Bioré, 186
blank-tape levy, 225
Blondie, 7
Born on a *Pirate Ship* (Barenaked Ladies), 137
Boston, 140
Bowie, David, 53
Branding, 173
Broken Social Scene, 237
Bush, Kate, 7, 79
By Divine Right, 237

C

Calgary, 203
Cambodia, 111, 177
Cameron, Deane, 54
Canning, Brendan, 237
Capital (records), 54
CDs
    enhanced, 227
    introduction of, 223–25
CBGB (club), 155
chant CDs, 203
Chapman, Tracy, 179, 180, 183
Chernobyl, 51
child prostitution, 111, 112
Choeung Ek killing fields (Cambodia), 112
Chris & Cosey, 76
Chulo Pony (clothing line), 234
Cinematica, 21
CIRPA, 213
CITR (radio), 21

City of Angels (film), 225
"City Sleeps, The" (MC 900 Ft. Jesus), 235
Clarkson, Kelly, 235
Cleveland, 54
Club Flamingo (Halifax), 65, 67
club scene, 54, 57
Cocteau Twins, 79
Cohen, Leonard, 65
Coldplay, 194, 207
Cole, Paula, 151, 152, 179
Colorado College, 237
Commonwealth Stadium, 204
consumers, behavioural shift, 223–24
Co-op radio, 33
copyright, 224, 226, 227
Coupland, Douglas, 29
Crash Test Dummies, 67, 121, 122
Crete, 129
Crompton, Kevin (cEvin), 29, 30, 51
Crow, Sheryl, 185
Cure, The, 30

D
Dalhousie University Student Union, 7
dance music, 29
"Dancing at the Feet of the Moon" (Luba), 91
Davis, Clive, 97, 98, 101, 223
de Burgh, Chris, 92
Dead Kennedys, 30, 33
Deep End, 102
Delerium, 232
Denver, John, 53
Depeche Mode, 33
Diamond, Marty, 97, 152, 155–56, 183, 185, 189
Dido, 167, 237
"Dig It" (Skinny Puppy), 51, 53
digital music model, 213, 215
Doors, The, 53
"Download This Song" (MC Lars), 226

downloads, 209, 213
drugs, 54, 55
Duff, Hillary, 235

E
E (band), 232
ego, 139, 201
eight-track tapes, 223
Elliot, Missy, 185
Eno, Brian, 92
"Everytime I See Your Picture" (Luba), 91

F
Fabri, Cliff, 165, 167
FACTOR, 213
Falwell, Jerry, 185
Fashion Dance concept, 29
Fiest, Leslie, 237
Fitzgerald, F. Scott, 235
Fonda, Jane, 51
FOXX (band), 232
France, Cathryn, 79
Fraser, Dan, 41, 119, 121, 126, 129, 131, 152, 155–56, 170, 209
Fraser, Diane, 186
Fraser, Elizabeth, 79
French Letters, 54
Front Line Assembly, 232
Fulber, Rhys, 232
Fumbling Towards Ecstasy (McLaughlin), 119, 149
fundraising. *See* philanthropy

G
Gabriel, Peter, 79, 105
Gevatsos, Andrew, 140
Germany, 121, 122
Gill (McBride), Kelly, 18, 21
Gilmore, Steven, 35, 53
"Girlfriend" (Lavigne), 234

Girlie Goddess Tour, 152, 179
Go! Records, 33
Goettel, Dwayne, 51
Goo Goo Dolls, 225
Gordon (Barenaked Ladies), 137
Gore, Al, 53
Gore, Tipper, 53
Gorge, the, 185
Grammy Awards, 51, 170, 186, 234
Grapes of Wrath, The, 27, 30, 54, 76, 119, 234, 237
Greubel, David, 226–27
Gums (tour manager), 57, 59

H
Halifax, 7, 30, 65, 67, 79, 81, 82, 88, 149
Harvard Business School, 214
Harvard, Blake, 235
Heald, Crystal, 111
"Heartbreaker" (Benatar), 185
Hill, Faith, 165
"Hockey Night in Canada theme song," 232
homophobia, 185
Hooper, Chris, 27, 234
Hooper, Tom, 27
House, Griffin, 235
Houston, Whitney, 98, 119
Hunt, Gillian, 27, 33, 35, 37, 79
Hynde, Chrissie, 185

I
"I Will Follow" (U2), 21
Iggy Pop, 98, 179
Images in Vogue, 29, 54
insects, album (SPK), 235
iPod, 215
iTunes, 213

J
Jackson, Dave, 54

Japan, 170, 173, 225
Jewel, 179
Joel, Billy, 98
Joplin, Janis, 98
Jowett, Mark, 25–37, 101, 165, 167
Jowett, Paul, 37, 232
Joy Division, 33
Juno Awards, 234

K
K/Catherii, 234
Kane, Kevin, 27, 82
Kenny G, 98
Khmer Rouge, 112
Kinky, 237
kirtan artists, 203
"Kiss Me" (Sixpence None the Richer), 165
Kitchen, The (New York), 59
Kraftwerk, 33
Kreviazuk, Chantal, 235
Krongard, Ken, 167

L
Lady Gaga, 207
Ladytron, 237
Lanois, Daniel, 92, 105
Lava Hay (band), 234
Lavigne, Avril
    awards, 170
    biggest-selling album, 234
    celebrity, 170, 173
    clothing line, 234
    downloads, 226
    early career, 165
    fundraising concerts, 203
    image, 163, 170
    leaves Nettwerk, 207
    marriage, 235
    personality, 165, 170

signs with Nettwerk, 170, 234
  tours, 173
Lavigne, Judy, 165, 167, 170
lawsuits, 151, 226
Leeb, Bill, 232
Let Go (Lavigne), 170, 234
Lilith Fair, 203, 204, 207
  artists, 179–80, 185, 186
  bomb threats/protests, 185
  corporate sponsorship, 185, 189
  dollar-per-ticket commitment, 189, 191
  first concert, 152, 155–56
  founding of, 151–52
  media coverage, 179, 180, 183, 185, 186, 189, 235
  merchandise, 186
  number of shows, 235
  nicknames, 180
  philanthropy, 183, 189, 191, 237
  ticket prices, 189
  top-grossing festival, 235
Lilith backstory, 179–80, 183
Limited Vision, 82
Little Big Man (talent agency), 183
locked master, 215
Lollapalooza, 179
Loeb, Lisa, 152
Los Angeles, 155, 165, 173, 185
Los Angeles Galaxy Major League Soccer Club, 237
Lott, Roy, 223
Luba, 91, 92
Luv-a-Fair (club), 33, 35, 43

M
macho hierarchy, 185
MacLean, Tara, 235
Maddalozzo, Joe, 53
Madrigal Press, 234
MAMA Group, 203
Manilow, Barry, 98

Mann, Aimee, 152, 155
Marchand, Pierre, 91, 92, 95, 97, 101–2, 105, 191
Maruyama, Tonni, 85
mass marketing, 119
Matrix, The, 165
MC 900 Ft. Jesus, 235, 237
MC Lars, 226
McBride, Jack, 1, 17, 18, 43, 76, 191
McBride, Pat, 18
McBride, Terry
  approach to artists, 177
  childhood, 17–18, 21
  co-founds Nettwerk, 35, 37
  consumer-behaviour perspective, 223–25
  divorce, 207
  early ventures, 18, 33
  education, 21, 191
  family. *See* Barrett McBride, Cathy; Barrett McBride, Kai; Barrett McBride, Mira
  futurist perspective, 209, 215
  impact of Lilith on, 204
  intuitive sense, 224
  love of music, 21, 209
  marketing methodology, 29, 35, 119, 121, 137, 139, 140, 143, 170, 173, 219
  and new technology, 218–19, 223
  personality, 76, 102, 137, 207
  philanthropy, 189, 191
  physical appearance, 65, 76, 137
  relationship with father, 17, 18, 43, 191
  self-reflection, 207
  song as emotion concept, 209, 225
  vision, 137, 140, 143
  work ethic, 17, 18, 76, 135
  yoga practice, 203–4, 209
McGarrigle, Anna, 92
McGarrigle, Kate, 92
McLaughlin, Jack, 76
McLaughlin, Sarah

American label, 97–98
awards, 234
biggest single, 232
carpets, 155, 156, 185
death of mother, 207
divorce, 207
first album, 85
first concert, 7–8, 11
image, 97–98
lawsuit, 151
obsessive-fan incident, 151
on songwriting, 79, 82
papal Christmas concert, 126, 129, 131
  personal philosophy, 117
  personality, 63, 67, 69, 105, 122
  philanthropy, 203, 232 (*See also* Lilith Fair)
  politics of, 131
  relationship with mother, 7, 102
  soundtracks, 225
  teenage years, 8, 11
  trip to Thailand/Cambodia, 111–12, 117, 177
  vegetarianism, 129
  work ethic, 15
micro-marketing, 119, 121
millennium generation, 223
Milwaukee, 54, 119
Mind—The Perpetual Intercourse (Skinny Puppy), 53
Moev, 7, 29, 30, 33, 35, 43, 79, 91, 232
Montreal, 54, 91, 92
Moore, Mandy, 235
MOR (middle of the road), 98
Morissette, Alanis, 215
Morocco, 126, 129
Morris, Madeline 232
Mott the Hoople, 53
MP3, 213, 215
Much Music, 111
Mulligan, Terry David, 111
Mushroom Studios, 53, 237

music business, changing, 207, 209, 213, 223–24
music executives vs. artists, 227
music videos, 225
Myers, Mike, 234
Myers, Paul, 234

N
Napster, 213, 225
Netflux, 224
Nettwerk–Arista relationship, 167
Nettwerk artists, 230–31
Nettwerk locations, 237
Neudorf, Darryl, 82, 149
New Orleans, 105
New York, 54, 59, 165, 183
Newbury Comics, 140
Nick of Time (Raitt), 186
Noetix, 33
North by Northeast music conference, 165
Nutone, 203

O
O'Connor, Sinead, 79, 185
October Game (band), 7
Odyssey Imports, 21, 30, 33, 53, 79
Ogilvie, Kevin ("Ogre"), 29, 30, 51, 53
"Oh, Little Town of Bethlehem," 129, 131
"Old Apartment, The" (Barenaked Ladies), 139
Old Crow Medicine Show, 235
Olympic Canadian Field Hockey Team, 237
"One Week" (Barenaked Ladies), 232
Ozzfest, 179

P
Page, Steven, 137, 139
Parents' Music Resource Center, 53
Paris, 122, 125–26, 129, 131
payola, 218
philanthropy, 51, 177, 89, 191, 203

Phillips, Darren, 82
Phnom Penh (Thailand), 111
Pine Knob Amphitheatre (Detroit), 152, 155
Pittsburg, 185
"Possession" (McLaughlin), 151
Pretenders, The, 185
Prince, 185
Public Eye Sound, 54
punk rock, 29

Q
QuickTime, 223

R
Radio Ethiopia tour, 152
Raitt, Bonnie, 186
Reagan, Ronald, 51
recession (2010), 209
Recording Industry Association of America (RIAA), 224, 226, 227
Reely, Greg, 27, 53, 54, 82
Reid, Antonio "LA," 167
Revelle, Graham, 235
right-to-life movement, 185
Roberts, Oral, 237
Robertson, Ed, 135, 137, 139–40, 143
Robertson, Hannah, 139
Robertson, Natalie, 139
Rock Spectacle (Barenaked Ladies), 139, 140
Rolling Stone, 51, 204
Rough Trade, 35
Roxy Music, 237
Rummen, John, 140

S
Saltzberg, Brad, 30, 33
Saltzberg, Herman, 30, 33
Saltsberg, Shaw, 147, 218–19
San Francisco, 33, 43

Saputo, Sheila, 237
Saskatoon, 219
Sgt. Pepper's Lonely Hearts Club Band (Beatles), 53
"Shoebox" (Barenaked Ladies), 139
"Silence" (McLaughlin), 232
Simon & Garfunkel, 79
Simple Minds, 33
Singapore, 173
Sixpence None the Richer, 165
"Sk8er Boi" (Lavigne), 226
Skinny Puppy, 29, 30, 33, 51, 54, 57, 59, 65, 232
Slade, 53
Smith, Fred "Sonic," 155
Smith, Jackson, 155
Smith, Patti, 98, 152, 155–56
Soft Rock Café (Vancouver), 54
Solace (McLaughlin), 105
song as emotion concept, 209, 225
Sood, Ash, 180, 207
SoundScan, 119, 218, 219
soundtracks, 225
Spears, Britney, 165
SPK (Graham Revelle), 235
Stefani, Gwen, 235
Sting, 151
"Stripped" tour, 152
Stunt (Barenaked Ladies), 140, 235
Submarines, 235
Sum 41, 203
Supremes, The, 53
Surfacing (McLaughlin), 225
Sweet, 53
Sweret, Richard, 97

T
Taiwan, 173
technological age, 218
Teletubby Tinky Winky, 185
Thailand, 111, 177

Thatcher, Margaret, 51
"That's What Friends Are For" (Bacharach/Bayer Sager), 51
The, The, 33
This Mortal Coil, 79
Thomas, Rosie, 237
Time magazine, 204, 235
Tokyo, 170, 173
Toronto, 54, 85, 165
Touch (McLaughlin), 85, 95, 102, 151
Toulyev (Moev), 30
"Trauma Hound" (Skinny Puppy), 59
Trobbin Gristle, 29
tsunami (2004), 203
Turtles, The, 53
Tyler, Steve, 101

U
U2, 21
Underwood, Carrie, 235
Union Carbide, 51
United Kingdom, 170
University of British Columbia (UBC), 21, 54, 235

V
Vancouver, 7, 29, 33, 35, 54, 57, 69, 75, 79, 85, 98, 101, 165, 170, 203, 207, 219, 232, 237
Vancouver Province and UBC Battle of the Battle of the Bands, 54
Vatican, 126, 129, 131
Vega, Suzanne, 179
videos. See music videos
vinyl, 209, 213
violence against women, 189
"Vox" (McLaughlin), 85, 97

W
Wailers, the, 65
Warner Brothers, 225
Warped Tour, 179, 185

Washburn, Abigail, 237
Watson, Doc, 235
Wax Trax, 35
"We Are the Galaxy" (Kinky), 237
Whibley, Deryck, 235
Wild Sky (studio), 91, 95, 101
women, charities benefiting, 204 (*See also* Lilith Fair)
women's shelters, 189, 191
World Records, 43
World Vision, 111

Y
yoga, 203, 204, 209

Z
Zappa, Frank, 53
Zizzo, Peter, 165, 167